Whispers Amongst Delegates

Anas Dhorajiwala

INDIA · SINGAPORE · MALAYSIA

ISBN 979-8-89133-795-4

To my friends and readers, thank you for your enthusiasm and patience. And to my family, who have always believed in my tales of love and passion, thank you for being my anchor.

CONTENTS

Part III

Part IV

Part I

Swaying Flags, Syncing Hearts

Mumbai, the city of dreams. The relentless monsoon rain drummed against the windows, making the city appear as though it was painted with watercolors. The aroma of wet earth mixed with the distant scent of street food, as the bustling metropolis welcomed delegates from all corners of the globe for the International Model United Nations Conference.

Elena Rosales was adjusting her papers in her hotel room overlooking the iconic Marine Drive. Her brunette hair, pulled back into a neat ponytail, contrasted starkly against her fair complexion. The salty breeze from the Arabian Sea playfully rustled the curtains, but Elena's blue eyes betrayed a storm of emotions: excitement, nervousness, and ambition. Her roommate, Isabella, glanced at her with an amused smile, "Nervous much? Remember, today's just the inaugural ceremony."

Elena nodded, her gaze distant, "I know, Isabella. But representing Mexico in India, that too in Mumbai? It's surreal."

Aarav Mehta, meanwhile, navigated the city's crowded streets, the rhythm of the raindrops syncing with his heartbeat. He was an embodiment of Mumbai – a blend of tradition and modernity. His deep-set brown eyes usually held a story, and today they were filled with determination. Glancing at his watch, he realized he might be late.

He quickly texted his friend, Ritesh, "Almost there! Hope they haven't started."

The conference venue, a grand hall with ornate Indian designs, was a testament to the country's rich heritage. The room buzzed with anticipation and the cacophony of multiple languages. Entering the venue, Elena felt a rush of exhilaration. The bright saris, the eloquence of the speakers, the gravity of the conference, it was overwhelming. She took a deep breath, trying to calm her nerves.

Then, a voice interrupted her thoughts, "Is this seat taken?"

She looked up, meeting Aarav's gaze. For a brief second, time seemed to pause. The sounds around them faded, and all that remained was the unspoken connection between two strangers. With a shy smile, Elena responded, "It's all yours."

As the ceremony proceeded, amidst the vibrant display of cultures and the symphony of languages, two hearts in the vast hall began to beat in sync. The Mumbai monsoons, known to weave countless tales of romance, had just embarked on narrating another.

The ceremony's grandeur was unmistakable. A large dais at the front was decorated with the flags of every participating nation, fluttering gently under the soft spotlight. A banner overhead read, "Welcome to the International Model United Nations Conference - Mumbai 2023." The event organizers had ensured that every detail, from the backdrop to the seating arrangements, exuded the essence of a genuine United Nations meet.

A soft murmur of anticipation filled the room as the delegates settled down. Elena, trying to appear composed, turned to Aarav, "Is this your first MUN?"

Aarav chuckled, "Hardly. Mumbai hosts a lot of these, and I've been part of a few. But an international MUN? This is a first. How about you?"

Elena's eyes sparkled, "I've attended a couple back in Mexico. But the atmosphere here? It's electric!"

As the chatter continued, the lights dimmed, and the ceremony began. A classical Indian dance performance narrating the story of unity and diversity mesmerized the audience. The intricacy of the footwork and the dancers' colorful attire left Elena awestruck.

Following the dance, the conference's chief organizer, Mrs. Lakshmi Menon, took the stage. Her authoritative yet kind voice echoed in the hall. "Ladies and gentlemen, welcome to Mumbai and to this year's International Model United Nations Conference. It is heartening to see young minds, future leaders, gathered here, all driven by a passion for global issues and diplomacy. "She continued, "For those new to MUNs, allow me to give a brief overview. Model United Nations, or MUN, is a simulation of the actual

United Nations where students role-play as delegates from different countries. They debate, deliberate, and work together to resolve pressing global issues. Today, you're not just students; you are representatives of nations. Your words carry weight, your actions have consequences, and your decisions shape the course of this simulation. But remember, the friendships and connections you make here are very real." The auditorium filled with applause. Elena felt a rush of pride and anticipation. The weight of responsibility and the exhilaration of the event were palpable.

Aarav leaned in, whispering to Elena, "It never gets old. The thrill, the passion, the responsibility. Every MUN is a new journey."

Elena nodded, smiling in agreement, "And what a journey this promises to be." The ceremony continued with an outline of the topics to be discussed over the week, ranging from climate change to global peacekeeping. As the delegates listened, both Elena and Aarav felt the gravity of the discussions that lay ahead. But amidst the seriousness, the budding camaraderie between them was undeniable. As the inaugural ceremony drew to a close, the delegates were left with a mix of anticipation and excitement for the sessions to come. But for Elena and Aarav, the MUN was not just about diplomacy and debates. The city of Mumbai, with its vibrant colors, relentless rains, and timeless tales, had set the stage for a story of their own.

The next morning, as the delegates trickled into the conference room, the air was thick with expectation. Each individual represented a nation, and with it, the aspirations, grievances, and hopes of its people. Aarav, representing

India, took his place alongside Elena, who was Mexico's voice. The buzz of conversations quickly filled the room as delegates discussed strategy, formed alliances, and anticipated opposition.

Aarav leaned towards Elena, his voice low, "The topic for today is 'Climate Change and its Global Impacts'. With the recent events and the international outcry, it promises to be a heated debate."

Elena nodded, her brow furrowing. "There's a lot at stake. Developing countries like mine are facing the brunt of climate change, but we need the developed nations on board to make substantial changes."

The session was officially called to order by the chairperson, Mr. Desai, a renowned figure in the world of international relations and a professor at a prominent Mumbai university. "Delegates," he began, "the issues you discuss and the resolutions you propose will not only reflect your understanding of international law but also your commitment to global peace and cooperation."

A delegate from the USA was the first to speak, emphasizing the need for shared responsibility while reminding the assembly of America's recent initiatives in renewable energy. The delegate from China followed, speaking about the balance between industrial growth and environmental conservation.

As the discussion progressed, Aarav took the floor. "The Indian subcontinent," he began, "faces both the challenge and opportunity in the fight against climate change. While we strive for development, it's imperative to remember our age-old ethos of harmony with nature. The Vedas have long spoken of the Earth as a mother, and it's high time we all treat her as such." He went on to discuss India's strategies and the need for technology transfer and fair trade practices to combat climate change effectively.

Elena listened intently, making notes. When her turn came, she stood tall, her voice filled with emotion. "Mexico," she started, "faces the wrath of nature every year with increasing hurricanes and changing rain patterns. But we are resilient. We seek collaboration, not charity. We ask for understanding and a chance to voice the concerns of the many nations that suffer silently." She emphasized the importance of international law in ensuring that all nations, big or small, had a voice and a chance at a sustainable future.

The room filled with applause as Elena concluded. There were many voices, many opinions, and underlying it all, the intricate web of international relations. Nations might have borders, but problems like climate change knew none. Solutions required collective action, understanding, and most importantly, empathy.

During a break, Elena and Aarav stepped out to the balcony, overlooking Mumbai's skyline, shimmering under the monsoon drizzle. "You were brilliant in there," Aarav said, admiration evident in his voice.

Elena smiled, "So were you. It's inspiring to see so many young minds passionate about these issues. But more than the debates, it's the connections we make, the perspectives we gain, that truly matter."

Aarav nodded in agreement. The MUN was indeed a microcosm of the world's political stage, a chance for the youth to engage in matters of global importance.

But for Elena and Aarav, amidst the debates and laws, a different kind of connection was taking root, one that neither had anticipated but both were beginning to cherish.

The morning's intense session seemed to lighten up post the morning tea break. It was no longer just about policies and official stances. The room turned into a melting pot of personalities.

"Point of Information," a delegate from Brazil stood up and inquired, only to ask, "Is it true that the samosas during the break were vegan?" The room erupted in laughter. Even Mr. Desai, the chairperson, couldn't contain a smile. "Let's save the culinary queries for lunchtime, delegate," he said, chuckling. A delegate from Sweden, known for her poetic prowess, took the floor next. "In the land of the midnight sun, we stand, seeking solutions under this Mumbai sun. Climate change is real, my friends, not some fairy tale. If we don't act now, we might as well be chasing our tail." The room filled with applause, some for the message, some for her impromptu rhyming.

The committee being simulated was the United Nations Framework Convention on Climate Change (UNFCCC). Every year, this committee attracted delegates who were passionate about the environment and sustainable growth. And this year was no different.

During a moderated caucus on the impact of climate change on biodiversity, the delegate from Australia began his speech, "As we speak, our beloved kangaroos back home might be wondering if their boxing gloves need to be traded for swimsuits."

The delegate from Japan whispered to his neighbor, representing the UK, "If climate change was a game, it'd be Jumanji. Every year, a new challenge!"

The UK delegate grinned, scribbling something on a piece of paper before passing it over. It was a doodle of Earth wearing sunglasses with a caption: "Too hot to handle?" Amid the laughter and lighter moments, the Executive Board, consisting of Mr. Desai and two other experts in international law and environmental science, guided the delegates, ensuring that discussions remained constructive and resolutions were formed. They played the dual role of educators and regulators, steering the ship of the conference smoothly.

Towards the end of the day's session, a delegate from Canada stood up, slightly nervous. "Honorable chair, fellow delegates," he began, his voice shaky. Looking down at his notes and then up again, he continued, "With great power comes... Uhm... great... responsibility? No wait, that's Spiderman. I meant... with great industrialization comes great... Ugh, never mind."

Elena nudged Aarav, whispering, "Looks like he's been watching too many movies during lockdown."Aarav chuckled, "I guess we all have our ways of dealing with stress. International law one day, Spiderman quotes the next."

As the gavel marked the end of the session 1, the delegates left the room with a mix of satisfaction and anticipation for the discussion ahead post. They had not only debated global issues but had also formed bonds over shared humor, poetic musings, and a deep-seated desire to make a difference.

The delegates returned from lunch, the hum of conversations revealing that alliances had started forming. The backdrop of Mumbai's iconic skyline from the conference room window added gravitas to the afternoon's session, with the distant cityscape washed clean by the monsoon rains.

As the session resumed, the delegate from Nigeria, a tall and imposing figure with a deep voice, commanded the room's attention. "Distinguished Chair, fellow delegates, the impact of climate change isn't a potential threat; it's a lived reality for millions. While we break for samosas and chai, my country battles with the consequences of desertification. This is an urgent cry for help." A hushed silence followed. The playful atmosphere from the morning session had shifted to a more pressing tone.

The delegate from Russia, a woman known for her sharp analytical skills, interjected, "While I sympathize with the delegate from Nigeria, it's imperative that we recognize this is a global issue. Let's discuss actionable solutions rather than laying blame."

"I don't recall placing blame," the Nigerian delegate replied tersely, "but while we're on the subject, developed nations should acknowledge their larger role in creating this crisis."Aarav, sensing the temperature of the room rising both literally and metaphorically, took a deep breath and stood. "Honorable chair," he began, choosing his words carefully, "We are all here because we care about our planet. While historical responsibility is essential, it's equally vital that we look forward and come up with collaborative solutions."

Elena, equally impassioned, stood next. "Climate change doesn't respect borders. The melting glaciers don't stop and think, 'Oh, let's not flood this country because they have lower carbon emissions.' We need to act as one."

The room broke into applause, recognizing the sentiment behind her words. Suddenly, a delegate from Chile stood, visibly flustered, "If we don't address the socio-economic impacts of climate change alongside the environmental ones, we are merely putting a band-aid on a bullet wound!"

This comment set the stage for more intense discussions on international laws surrounding climate change, compensation, adaptation, and mitigation. Delegates referenced the Paris Agreement, the Kyoto Protocol, and other international legislations, striving to navigate the maze of responsibilities, rights, and reparations.

As the day's discussions grew more heated, Mr. Desai intervened, "Let's remember, we're here as ambassadors of hope. While our countries may have differing views, we all share the same home - Earth. Let's ensure we leave today having taken a step forward, however small."

Aarav caught Elena's eye across the room. Both seemed to have the same thought - this MUN was turning out to be more intense than they had imagined. But beneath that intensity was the budding realization that these debates, these discussions, were shaping them, preparing them for a world that urgently needed leaders, visionaries, and above all, compassionate humans. Mr. Desai's attempt to soothe the heightened emotions worked momentarily, but as the session progressed, a new topic emerged, a dilemma that has baffled policymakers for decades: The balance between the Right to Development and the Right to a Healthy Environment. The delegate from

Brazil was the first to touch upon the subject. "Our nation, like many others, is still developing. While we recognize and understand the importance of environmental conservation, we cannot deny our people their right to development, to pull millions out of poverty."

Elena, ever the environmentalist, stood immediately after. "The Right to a Healthy Environment is fundamental. We cannot use the excuse of development to decimate forests, poison rivers, and destroy the very land we call home. We must find a way to develop sustainably."Aarav, on the other hand, resonated with the developing nations' plight. "Sustainable development is indeed the future. However, developed nations reached their zenith by exploiting natural resources during their time. Developing nations are merely asking for a level playing field. Isn't it hypocritical to deny them their right?"

Elena, slightly taken aback by Aarav's stand, countered, "We're in the age of technology and information. There are sustainable methods available now that weren't known during the industrial revolution. We can't use historical actions as an excuse for present recklessness." A delegate from Germany interjected, "The International Covenant on Economic, Social, and Cultural Rights has enshrined the Right to Development. It's a recognized international law." "Yes," Elena shot back, "But what about the Stockholm Declaration, or the Rio Declaration? Both of these emphasize the fundamental right to a healthy environment."

Aarav added, "The UN Declaration on the Right to Development also explicitly mentions that development should aim at the constant improvement of well-being of the entire population. Isn't the environment a part of this?"

The debate grew fierce. References were made to numerous international treaties, conventions, and laws. Delegates cited the Aarhus Convention, the Espoo Convention, and the International Law Commission's draft principles on the protection of the environment in relation to armed conflicts.

It was evident that the balance between environmental protection and the right to development was not an easy one. As the day's session neared its end, the room was thick with tension. Mr. Desai, seeing the need to calm things, intervened, "Thank you, everyone, for the passion and knowledge you've brought to today's discussions. This is the spirit of MUN. Remember, it's not about winning; it's about understanding different perspectives."

Elena and Aarav exchanged a tense glance. Both had come to appreciate the depth of the other's convictions, but it was clear their budding friendship was going to be tested by their differing worldviews.

As the debate intensified, the ambient hum of whispers grew louder. The delegate from South Africa passionately argued for the right to development, emphasizing the economic disparities between the global North and South. "Historical oppressions have left many nations in a developmental limbo. You cannot deny our people their rightful climb out of poverty!" Several delegates from African and Asian nations nodded in agreement, their hands thumping their desks in approval – a common form of applause in the Model UN world. Elena, refusing to back down, stood, her eyes flashing with defiance. “While I understand the need for development, we are now on the brink of environmental collapse! It’s not just about historical mistakes; it’s about the future. We need to prevent a catastrophe, not push our planet to the edge!”

Aarav, looking more intense than Elena had ever seen him, countered, “Delegate It’s easy for developed nations to talk about environment conservation when they’ve already achieved their development. The rest of us are still trying to provide basic amenities to our people. Every nation has the right to its developmental journey.”

Several delegates from developed nations seemed uncomfortable, shifting in their seats. Whispers turned into hushed debates among blocs. Some delegates scribbled furiously on notepads, passing notes and forming strategies. The “Right to Development” bloc, which Aarav was subtly leading, was growing in number, consolidating their arguments. Elena, feeling isolated but resolute, rallied her troops. The “Right to a Healthy Environment” bloc, although smaller in number, was vociferous. “How can you talk about development when there might not be a planet left to develop?” she posed, challenging Aarav directly. A delegate from Australia chimed in, “While we respect the right to development, we must also recognize the catastrophic impacts of climate change. Sea levels are rising, wildfires are increasing, and coral reefs are dying!”

Aarav added, “True, but India’s National Green Tribunal has been making strides in balancing environmental conservation with developmental needs. Every nation can find its equilibrium.” The debate took a light-hearted turn when a delegate from Canada said, "If we don't solve this, our future will just be us, floating on icebergs, saying 'I told you so' to each other." A ripple of laughter spread through the room.

But the levity was short-lived. Delegates exchanged barbed comments, cited international laws, and referenced past resolutions. There was a dramatic moment when a delegate quoted Gandhi: "The world has enough for everyone's need but not for everyone's greed."

As the day neared its end, the room's atmosphere was electric. Elena and Aarav, while respecting each other's intellect, were at loggerheads. The gavel signaled the end of the session, but it was clear that the battle lines were drawn, and the real debate was only just beginning.

* * * * *

Sparks and Speeches

As the tension in the room reached its zenith, the chair of the Executive Board announced, "Given the passion and dedication displayed today, we have a unique proposal. A 1v1 challenge between two of our most vocal delegates. India and Mexico, a direct exchange of views on our platform. Five minutes each, no interruptions."

The room buzzed with anticipation. Such a challenge was rare, but not unheard of in MUNs. Elena, though taken by surprise, nodded her acceptance, her posture radiating determination. Aarav, a mix of intrigue and challenge in his eyes, agreed.

As murmurs and whispers echoed throughout the committee room, the chair's voice cut through, "We are now proceeding with the one-on-one challenge between the delegate of India and the delegate of Mexico. Each will have five minutes to put forth their arguments. Given the gravity of this session, I urge all to maintain decorum."

Aarav rose from his seat, a sheaf of papers in hand, taking measured steps to the podium. He began, "Honorable chair, distinguished delegates, and particularly, the delegate of Mexico, the right to development, enshrined in the Declaration on the Right to Development adopted by the UNGA in 1986, guarantees the inalienable right to economic, social, cultural, and political development, where all human rights and fundamental freedoms can be fully realized."

He continued, "The fervor of our discourse, the beauty of this deliberation, reminds me of Wordsworth's 'Daffodils.' Just as the poet found solace in the memory of the golden flowers, nations like mine seek solace in the promise of development. A promise to our citizens, to our youth, and to the numerous entrepreneurs and businesses eager to be a part of the global community."

Elena's eyes never left Aarav as she listened, formulating her response. When Aarav concluded, "Development is not just a want, it's a fundamental right," she was ready.

Rising gracefully, she began, "Delegate of India, while I admire the eloquence, I must draw attention to another fundamental right, the right to a healthy environment. This was recognized by the UN Human Rights Council in 2017. Both rights do not exist in isolation. It is a symbiotic relationship, much like Neruda's poetic words, where love and desire are intertwined, so are the rights of development and a healthy environment."

She leaned forward, "Might I remind the delegate of India about the Stockholm Declaration of 1972 or the Rio Declaration of 1992? Both conventions emphasize that environmental protection is an integral part of the development process. Sustainable development isn't a choice; it's a necessity."

Pausing for effect, she added, "But let's not forget, dear delegate, the role of businesses. Companies worldwide, from Tesla to Reliance, are adapting to a green future. Why? Not just for profit, but for the planet. The very planet our future generations will inherit. "The delegate of India speaks of promises. I urge him to promise a sustainable future, where both our rights are respected and fulfilled," the room erupted in applause.

Aarav with passion stating "The pursuit of development is not just about economic growth. It's about the right of a nation to uplift its people, to provide them with a life of dignity, security, and opportunity."

Elena, following him, retorted, "We are not anti-development. We are for sustainable development. What's the point of erecting skyscrapers if the very foundation, our earth, is crumbling beneath?"

As the allotted time for each neared its end, the delegates hung onto every word, the room's atmosphere thick with anticipation. As Elena concluded, the chair was about to interject when a note was passed to him.

He read it aloud, "In light of the intensity of today's debate and the passionate exchange between our delegates from India and Mexico, we will adjourn the session for the day."

A collective gasp ran through the room. Such abrupt endings were uncommon. The delegates, still processing the day's events, began packing their things.

The vice-chair added, "But the evening isn't over for our esteemed delegates. Remember, tonight we have the International Cultural Exchange Evening, a social event. Let's take off our delegate hats and get to know each other beyond the debates. See you all at the Grand Ballroom at 8 PM."

The evening held promise, not just of entertainment but of unpredictable interactions. Would the evening's events soften the intense rivalry between Aarav and Elena? The ballroom awaited.

Only time would tell.

* * * * *

Aarav entered his hotel room, still ruminating on the day's events. He found his roommate, Ritesh, sprawled on his bed, lazily scrolling through his phone. Ritesh was a delegate representing Brazil in the World Health Committee.

"Quite the show you put on there," Ritesh remarked, glancing up, a grin on his face.

Aarav sighed, loosening his tie, "I didn't expect it to get so heated, especially not on the first day."

Ritesh sat up, "That delegate from Mexico – Elena, was it? She's formidable. But you held your ground well."

"Thanks," Aarav replied, though his face reflected his inner turmoil. "But I have to win this. That scholarship to Stanford's international relations program is a dream. You know how much it means to me, especially with our financial situation."

Ritesh nodded sympathetically. "You'll get it. Just don't let emotions override your diplomacy."

Across the corridor in another room, Elena was in a similar discussion with her roommate, Isabella, who was participating in the Economic and Financial Committee as the delegate of Spain.

Elena flopped down on her bed. "He's good, Isa. I mean, the delegate of India. He knows his conventions and laws, but there's an underlying passion, almost like poetry in motion."

Isabella, who was meticulously arranging her research papers, chuckled. "Sounds like someone's impressed."

Elena rolled her eyes, "It's not about being impressed. It's about understanding the competition. Winning this MUN means the scholarship to Stanford for me. After all the work and preparation, I can't afford to lose, not when it's this close."

Isabella came over and sat next to Elena, "Hey, it's just the first day. You've got this. And who knows, maybe this competition will give way to something more... interesting between you two."

Elena smirked, "Let's not get ahead of ourselves. For now, it's about the debate and that scholarship."

Both rooms were filled with the same determination. The stakes were high, and the journey had just begun.

Elena stared up at the ceiling, her hands cushioning the back of her head. There was something about Aarav that gnawed at her. The intensity with which he debated, his unwavering gaze, and the subtle grace with which he enunciated each word. It was undeniably magnetic.

"Are you okay?" Isabella's voice cut through Elena's thoughts.

Elena sighed. "You know, Isa, for all his knowledge about the international conventions and the fiery speeches, there's a vulnerability to him. It's like... he's pushing himself to the edge for something more than just the win."

Isabella smirked, "Are we still talking about the debate or something else?"

Elena playfully nudged her roommate. "Oh, stop it! I just admire his conviction. But it's also intimidating. The fact that he can quote Neruda and then switch to discussing the intricacies of the Law of the Sea Convention, it's... impressive."

Isabella leaned closer, her playful grin widening, "You do realize you're smiling while talking about him, right?"

Elena groaned, her face turning a light shade of pink. "Fine, he's attractive, okay? But it doesn't change the fact that I have to best him in the committee."

Back in Aarav's room, Ritesh was observing Aarav's contemplative silence with growing amusement.

"Thinking about tomorrow's strategy or the Mexican delegate?"

Aarav shot him a sidelong glance. "Why not both? She's a formidable opponent. Her grasp over the topics, her ability to rope in the likes of Keynes and Sen in economic arguments and seamlessly shifting to the clauses of international environmental treaties... she's brilliant."

Ritesh grinned, teasingly, "And beautiful?"

Aarav laughed, "Super smart for her own good and yes, undeniably captivating. But don't you dare read too much into it."

The night wore on, and as both Aarav and Elena prepared for the the event which was now only an hour away, the ballroom socials.

The lavish ballroom was a sight to behold: sparkling chandeliers that cascaded a golden hue, a live orchestra playing a gentle waltz, and tables draped in ivory cloth with tall candelabras emitting a soft, romantic light. Delegates from various countries were now dressed in their finest attires, representing a blend of international sophistication and cultural distinctiveness.

Elena, looking resplendent in a midnight blue gown inspired by the traditional Mexican Tehuana, spotted Aarav from across the room. He was attired in a well-fitted black tuxedo, his kurta beneath adding a touch of Indian elegance. Their eyes met, and Aarav raised his glass in a mock toast, his eyes twinkling mischievously.

"Well, Delegate of India," Elena said when they finally faced each other, a playful edge to her voice, "Didn't expect to see you here after that intense face-off. Thought you'd be preparing your next argumentative bombardment for tomorrow."

Aarav smiled, "Ah, Delegate of Mexico, even warriors need a break. Besides, isn't this what the Congress of Vienna was about? Wining, dining, and a little bit of diplomacy on the side?"

Elena laughed, "Touche. Though, I hope our resolutions are more effective than the Concert of Europe turned out to be."

Their banter continued, and it was evident to onlookers that there was an electric chemistry between the two. They danced a few steps, their movements mirroring their debate style—graceful yet intense.

As the music changed to a more contemporary beat, delegates cheered and began showcasing dance moves from their respective countries. Elena pulled Aarav into a Salsa, her laughter echoing over the music as he tried to match her steps, teasing him, "Come on, Delegate of India, keep up!"

Aarav smirked, drawing her closer, "If this were a dance-off, I'd say we're recreating the Cuban Missile Crisis - two superpowers coming dangerously close to a showdown."

Their dance concluded amid applause. They were breathless, the challenge of the dance floor mirroring the day's debates. Yet, amidst the humor, sarcastic remarks, and historical references, the connection between them was undeniable. But neither was ready to admit it. Not just yet.

* * * * *

The evening ended, and as delegates dispersed, Elena whispered to Isabella, "I can't believe I danced with him. But, there's just something about him, Isa."

Isabella grinned, "Something or someone, you mean?"

Elena rolled her eyes but couldn't suppress a smile. As for Aarav, he just looked back once at the ballroom's entrance, his gaze searching for Elena, and whispered to himself, "The plot thickens."

The anticipation for the next day's debates, combined with the underlying tension between Aarav and Elena, promised an eventful continuation of the conference.

Aarav had barely begun to unwind after the ball when he heard a soft rustling from his room. Cautiously, he approached, finding the door ajar. Pushing it open, he spotted the delegate of Pakistan hurriedly scanning a document on Aarav's desk – his draft resolution for the next day.

"Caught red-handed, Delegate!" Aarav barked, his eyes narrowing. "What business do you have in my room and with my papers?"

The delegate of Pakistan, Farhan, looked up, his face pale, realizing the gravity of his misstep. "Look, Aarav, it's not what you think."

Aarav took an intimidating step forward. "Oh, isn't it? Enlighten me then."

Farhan hesitated for a split second before blurting out, "The sustainable development bloc... they wanted an inside look at your strategies. They... they asked me to sneak a peek."

Aarav's fists clenched. "Are you implying Elena put you up to this?"

Farhan nodded frantically, "Yes! She's heading the bloc, isn't she? She wanted to be a step ahead."

His heart heavy with disappointment and a tinge of anger, Aarav warned, "If I find out you're lying about Elena, you'll regret this, Farhan. Leave. Now."

As Farhan scuttled out, a whirlwind of emotions engulfed Aarav. Betrayed, hurt, and angry, he threw himself into his research, ensuring that his strategies were foolproof. If Elena wanted a battle, he'd give her war.

He didn't want to believe Elena could stoop so low, but the evidence was right in front of him. "Trust no one in diplomacy," his mentor's words echoed in his ears.

Aarav didn't sleep that night. He revisited treaties, pored over international laws, and redrafted his resolution. By dawn, he had created an unbeatable argument.

But as the sun's first rays pierced the Mumbai skyline, he couldn't help but wonder if, amid this political chess game, he was losing something far more personal.

Elena stepped into her hotel room, the music and chatter from the ballroom still lingering in her ears. Her heels clicked against the marble floor as she made her way to the window. The glittering lights of Mumbai stretched out in front of her, but her thoughts were occupied with the striking delegate from India.

Aarav. The name seemed to have rooted itself in her mind. The intense debate earlier, their sarcastic banter referencing historic events, and the brief moments of genuine connection had left a deep impression on her.

She couldn't ignore the flutter in her heart every time their eyes met or the shiver down her spine when they shared a brief moment of understanding. But she also couldn't ignore the competitive spark between them.

"Is he trying to charm me for an advantage? Or does he...?" she thought, but the voice in her head didn't finish the sentence. Elena was known for her sharp mind, but she couldn't decode Aarav's intentions. And it scared her.

Sitting at her desk, she took a deep breath and began her preparations. She had a reputation to uphold. If she wanted to win the scholarship to that prestigious school in the USA, she had to give her best. Elena knew that Aarav was her toughest competitor. His vast knowledge of international conventions and laws made him an adversary not to be taken lightly.

Hours passed, papers scattered across the room, multiple tabs open on her laptop. Every now and then, her thoughts drifted back to Aarav. She wondered what he was doing, whether he was preparing as intensely as she was, or whether he was somewhere thinking about her.

The wee hours of the morning approached. Tiredness took its toll, but she pushed through. Elena knew that tomorrow would be crucial. She couldn't let her budding feelings for Aarav compromise her position. But there was a part of her, deep down, that hoped after all this was over, they could explore the "what ifs."

Unbeknownst to her, the events of the night would add another layer to their already complicated relationship.

* * * * *

The Tightrope of Trust

The morning sun streamed through the vast windows of the hotel's dining hall, casting a golden hue over the delegates as they began to gather for breakfast. There was a palpable tension in the air, a residual charge from the previous day's debates, exacerbated by the night's events, most of which remained hidden.

Elena entered the hall, scanning the room for familiar faces. She found some of her "sustainable development" bloc members seated at a table near the back. As she made her way there, she noticed Aarav at another table, deeply engrossed in a conversation with his bloc. His demeanor had visibly changed. The light-hearted, albeit competitive charmer from the ballroom seemed more serious and more formidable. He glanced up just as Elena passed by, their eyes meeting briefly. There was no warmth in his gaze, just a cold detachment. She felt a pang of confusion but quickly masked her emotions.

She joined her bloc, the talk immediately turning to strategies for the day. Whispers and hurried discussions filled the hall as different delegations huddled together. The weight of the impending debates, combined with the promise of the scholarship, made the atmosphere even more charged.

Aarav, leading his bloc, was a force to reckon with. Delegates from other countries approached him, seeking his advice or hoping to align with him. He discussed, planned, and commanded the room with a presence that was almost magnetic. Gone was the flirtatious banter from the previous day. This was a man on a mission, and everyone could feel it.

As the breakfast hour neared its end, Aarav stood up and made his way to the conference room. Elena watched him go, a mix of awe and concern in her eyes. She had always admired strong leaders, and Aarav's transformation was both intimidating and intriguing. The mysterious change in his behavior made her more determined to figure him out, even as she prepared to face him in the debate.

The delegates slowly started to filter out of the dining hall, heading towards the conference room. The battle lines were drawn, strategies set, and as the day progressed, it was clear that the MUN was about to witness one of its most intense sessions yet.

The hustle and bustle of the delegates filling the conference room quieted down as the Executive Board took their places. With a signal from the chairperson, the session began.

Elena adjusted her blazer and leaned in to converse with her bloc members, discussing last-minute changes to their resolution. But before they could even get their feet wet, Aarav stood up, requesting the floor to speak. With a nod from the chair, he began his address.

"Esteemed Chair, fellow delegates," Aarav began, a steely edge to his voice, "It is indeed ironic to hear the 'sustainable development' bloc, led by countries including Mexico, speak with such fervor about the urgency of development while their own nations grapple with inadequate funds to champion the cause they so passionately argue for."

The committee sat in rapt attention, some delegates glancing nervously at their papers, others exchanging concerned glances. Elena stiffened, immediately sensing the direction Aarav was heading.

Aarav continued, "India, as many of you are aware, is a signatory to the United Nations Framework Convention on Climate Change, and the Paris Agreement. We have shown commitment to reducing our carbon footprint, ensuring sustainable agriculture, and providing affordable and clean energy. We have set in motion significant projects aimed at both development and sustainability. Yet, it remains perplexing how the delegate of Mexico proposes methods of sustainable development that even their own country struggles to fund."

Murmurs filled the room, with some members of the 'sustainable development' bloc shifting uncomfortably in their seats.

"But let us not stray from the topic at hand," Aarav continued, his voice growing more powerful. "We are here to collaborate, not to tear each other down. If we wish to reach a consensus on sustainable development, it is vital to recognize and address the elephant in the room – the hypocrisy. While countries like India are making strides despite our challenges, we must ask: what is the 'sustainable development' bloc bringing to the table?"

Aarav paused for effect, letting his words hang in the air, his gaze finally settling on Elena. "Delegate of Mexico," he said, a challenge evident in his voice, "We are eager to hear your response."

The room was electrified, the tension palpable. Aarav had made his move, fearlessly and unapologetically. Elena took a deep breath, steadying herself. She had not anticipated such a fierce opening salvo from Aarav. But she was not one to back down, especially not with the stakes so high.

Taking a moment to collect her thoughts, Elena stood, preparing to counter Aarav's pointed arguments. The battle of wits and words had only just begun.

Elena, having been cornered by Aarav's audacious assertions, calmly and confidently began her rebuttal. "Esteemed Chair and fellow delegates, it is true that certain countries face challenges in funding sustainable development, but this very assembly is proof of our collective endeavor to collaborate and seek solutions."

She continued, "Mexico, along with other nations in our bloc, is actively seeking partnerships, creating policies, and exploring innovative financing mechanisms to overcome these challenges. It is easy to point out faults, but it is crucial to remember that sustainable development isn't a competition. It's a collective responsibility."

Aarav was quick to interject with a point of information, "Is the delegate of Mexico suggesting that nations with inadequate funds for sustainable development should lead the discourse on the same?"

Elena, maintaining her poise, responded, "Delegate of India, sustainable development is as much about intent as it is about finance. While funds are essential, vision, dedication, and a collaborative spirit also play an integral role. It's about quality, not just quantity."

Before Aarav could counter, the delegate of China took the floor, voicing support for India's stance but also highlighting the importance of nations like Mexico in global cooperation. The delegate of the USA chimed in, emphasizing the need for both development and environmental protection, drawing parallels with their own challenges and achievements.

The committee became a cauldron of passionate speeches, fervent defenses, and meticulous presentations, each country vying to place their perspective at the forefront. Delegates were constantly on their feet, making points, countering arguments, and seeking middle ground.

As the hours flew by, the morning's intensity only seemed to amplify. The back and forth was relentless. The Executive Board occasionally intervened, steering the discourse and ensuring decorum.

By the time the chair called for a lunch break, the atmosphere in the room was a mix of exhaustion and anticipation. Aarav and Elena exchanged brief glances – both their faces a mask, hiding their thoughts and strategies for the afternoon session.

As the delegates exited, conversations about the morning's fierce debates echoed through the corridors. Everyone was eagerly awaiting the afternoon's proceedings, wondering if common ground could ever be achieved between such staunch adversaries.

Elena paced the hallway, her heart heavy with the weight of the morning's debates. She could sense the palpable tension, the restrained aggression. But Aarav's indifference pained her more than the morning's face-off.

She decided to approach him, to clear the air. "Aarav," she called out as she hastened towards him. He didn't pause, continuing his brisk walk towards the conference cafeteria.

Undeterred, Elena decided to try again. Just as she was about to call out to him, Ritesh, a mutual friend from a previous MUN and a fellow delegate, intercepted her. His expression was somber.

"Elena," he began hesitantly, "I think you should know something."

She arched a brow, silently urging him to continue. Ritesh recounted the previous night's incident with the delegate of Pakistan, the suspicion towards the sustainable development bloc, and the misplaced blame on Elena.

Elena felt the blood drain from her face. The weight of understanding pressed upon her, leaving her breathless. "I had no idea," she whispered, shock evident in her voice. "Ritesh, you have to believe me. Neither I nor anyone from my bloc had any part in this."

Ritesh sighed, running a hand through his hair. "I believe you, Elena. But Aarav doesn't. He thinks you've played a dirty game to get ahead. He's taken this very personally."

Elena felt a lump form in her throat. "I need to win this MUN, Ritesh. Not just for the pride or the recognition, but there's so much riding on this for me. My family... they've invested everything in my education, hoping I'd get the scholarship to the USA. This is my chance to ensure a secure future for them. But I wouldn't stoop to such tactics."

Ritesh placed a reassuring hand on her shoulder. "I know you wouldn't. But Aarav is hurt, and when Aarav is hurt, he gets cold and reticent."

She blinked back tears of frustration. "I need to set things right."

"You will," Ritesh said, "but it's going to be a tough road ahead."

As the break came to an end, Elena braced herself for the forthcoming sessions, armed with renewed determination. She had two battles to fight now: one on the conference floor and another with her heart.

The grand hall echoed with whispers as the afternoon session of the conference began. This was no ordinary session; delegates were to face the International Press (IP). Reporters from various renowned international publications, representing a fictional media landscape, were in attendance, ready to grill the delegates.

Elena took her seat, noticing the gaunt look on Aarav's face. His usual confident demeanor had an underlying layer of fatigue, hinting at the previous sleepless night he'd endured.

"Ladies and gentlemen," began the IP head, "We will begin with the delegate of India." Cameras flashed as Aarav rose from his seat, proceeding to the center.

"Delegate of India," began a reporter with sharp features, "how do you respond to the accusations that your bloc is using aggressive tactics to bulldoze its way through the resolutions?"

Aarav, with a steely gaze, responded, "Our aim is to bring forth the realities that many choose to overlook. If stating facts and seeking accountability is seen as aggressive, then so be it."

The questions came rapidly after that. They touched on the technicalities of his resolutions, the financial aspects, and even his personal stance on several international issues. With each query, Aarav responded with the precision of a seasoned diplomat, his answers dripping with references to international law and historic events.

Elena, though part of the opposing bloc, couldn't help but admire Aarav's eloquence. She also noticed the subtle signs of his weariness — the occasional falter in his voice, the slight trembling of his hand as he sipped water.

Her turn at the podium was less intense. The questions were sharp, but not as numerous or aggressive as Aarav's. Her defense of the sustainable development bloc's approach was articulate, as she emphasized collaboration over conflict and the importance of securing a global future.

As the press conference drew to a close, a weight seemed to have lifted off everyone's shoulders. The day had been long, and the pressure intense. But for Aarav, it seemed doubly so. As he returned to his seat, Elena noticed the deep lines of exhaustion on his face.

The hall was abuzz with anticipation as the final committee session of the day commenced. Whispers floated around, speculating on the strategies each bloc would employ.

Aarav, struggling with his exhaustion, was trying his best to rally his bloc. He quickly went through his notes, scribbled down last-minute strategies, and whispered instructions to his allies.

Elena, sensing an opportunity, convened a huddle with her bloc members. She outlined a strategy that focused not only on counteracting Aarav's points but on building a compelling narrative for sustainable development. "We're not just here to win," she whispered to her team, "We're here to make a difference. Let's remind everyone why this is so crucial."

As she stepped up to the podium, the committee room went silent. Elena began her address by invoking the principles enshrined in international conventions. She talked about the Rio Declaration, Agenda 21, and the Sustainable Development Goals of the United Nations. With each point, she wove a narrative of the world's shared responsibility to protect the planet while ensuring growth.

Drawing on a wide range of data, she painted a vivid picture of the consequences of unchecked development, emphasizing the plight of vulnerable communities. "We must remember," she said, her voice firm, "that while we sit in these comfortable halls, debating resolutions, there are millions out there whose futures depend on the decisions we make today."

The room was captivated. Even delegates who had previously opposed her views found themselves nodding in agreement. Her words were a blend of hard facts, moral obligation, and a passionate plea for unity.

Aarav tried to interject with points of information. While they were relevant and sharp, his usual fervor seemed diminished. He struggled to keep his focus, the weight of his exhaustion evident in every word. His allies tried to rally, but the momentum was clearly with Elena and her bloc.

By the end of the session, it was clear that Elena had managed to sway a significant portion of the committee. While Aarav's points were valid and well-argued, Elena's combination of facts, passion, and impeccable timing had won the day.

As the delegates exited the hall, there was a sense of admiration for Elena. She had showcased her expertise, her dedication, and her leadership. But amidst the congratulations and smiles, her eyes searched for Aarav. She felt a pang of guilt seeing his exhausted figure slowly gathering his things. Her victory felt bittersweet. On one hand, she was proud of her achievements; on the other, she wished it hadn't come at the expense of someone she was growing fond of.

Elena found herself hesitating, torn between approaching Aarav or giving him space. On one hand, she wanted to clear the air, but on the other, she didn't want to push him further away.

* * * * *

Melodies and Skylines

The sprawling metropolis of Mumbai, with its blend of historic charm and modern vibrancy, awaited the delegates. The itinerary had scheduled a leisurely tour of the city's iconic landmarks, from the Gateway of India to Marine Drive's glittering seaface.

In Room 504 of the luxurious hotel, Aarav sat on the edge of his bed, his usually expressive eyes shadowed with exhaustion and introspection. His tie lay discarded on a chair, his sleeves rolled up. Ritesh, ever the concerned friend, tried to offer some words of comfort.

"You know, one session doesn't define the entire MUN. There's still another day," Ritesh began cautiously.

Aarav sighed, running a hand through his hair. "It's not just about the committee, Ritesh. It's... everything. The incident with the Pakistan delegate, the intensity of the debate, and now the surprise twist with Elena."

Ritesh frowned. "You think she had a hand in that?"

Aarav hesitated, "I don't want to believe it, but the thought keeps coming back. But seeing how today went, it doesn't seem like something she'd do. It's all confusing."

In the Room 712 was filled with a different energy. Elena was pacing, her thoughts a whirlwind. She had changed into casual attire for the tour but seemed far from ready. Her roommate, Isabella, watched her with a mix of amusement and concern.

"You're going to wear a hole in the carpet at this rate," Isabella remarked.

Elena halted, sending her a frustrated glance. "I just... I want to talk to Aarav. Explain things. But what if he doesn't want to listen? Or worse, what if he thinks I orchestrated the whole break-in?"

Isabella sighed, pulling Elena to sit down. "Look, from what you've told me about him, he seems reasonable. Maybe you should just talk it out. But, if you're really worried, perhaps meeting him outside of the conference setting would help."

Elena pondered this, her eyes lighting up. "You mean during the tour?"

Isabella nodded, a mischievous glint in her eyes. "Mumbai is the city of dreams, after all. Who knows? It might just be the perfect backdrop for mending bridges."

Elena smiled weakly, uncertainty still evident. "I hope so."

As both delegates prepared for the evening, a city of myriad experiences beckoned them. Whether the vibrant streets of Mumbai would help ease the tensions between them remained to be seen.

Downstairs in the grand lobby, the delegates buzzed with anticipation. As they chatted and laughed, waiting for the buses, Isabella caught Ritesh's arm.

"Hey," she said, flashing her most charming smile, "Is Aarav joining us for the tour?"

Ritesh gave a rueful chuckle, "He's decided to pass. Says he needs some downtime, especially after today."

Elena, overhearing their conversation, felt a pang of concern mixed with guilt. "I think I'll try to convince him to come. He shouldn't be alone now."

Ritesh looked surprised. "You sure that's a good idea?"

Elena squared her shoulders, her determination evident. "Yes."

With hurried footsteps, Elena made her way to the elevators, pressing the button for Aarav's floor. Every second felt like an eternity as the elevator ascended, her heart racing with a mixture of anxiety and hope.

She hesitated for a brief moment outside Room 504, took a deep breath, and knocked.

The door opened abruptly. To Elena's surprise, Aarav stood there, his well-defined muscles evident, his shirt absent. His dark eyes, filled with a mixture of irritation and fatigue, locked onto hers, causing her to momentarily forget her purpose.

Regaining her composure, Elena said, "I didn't expect you to be... um, shirtless."

Aarav raised an eyebrow, his voice dripping with sarcasm, "And I didn't expect you'd be knocking at my door. Did you come to sneak a peek at my new resolution?"

Despite the sting of his words, Elena noticed the flicker of vulnerability behind his eyes. "May I come in?" she asked gently.

After a moment of hesitation, Aarav stepped aside, allowing her into his room. The dim lighting and scattered papers bore testimony to the intensity of the past few hours.

Elena looked around, searching for words, while Aarav crossed his arms, waiting. The tension in the room was palpable.

Aarav's dark eyes, tinged red from fatigue and emotion, met Elena's with a cold intensity. He motioned for her to sit, but she chose to stand, her posture defiant yet sincere.

"I didn't have anything to do with the Pakistan delegate's actions," she began, her voice firm. "I know what was said, but I had no part in it. My bloc does things by the book. Always."

Aarav's lips twisted into a cynical smirk. "By the book? Really? After the way you played today? How can I trust anything you say?"

Elena's cheeks flushed with anger. "I am competitive, Aarav, but I play fair. The Sustainable Development bloc may be strategic, but we are not dishonest."

He sighed, rubbing his temples as though trying to ward off an impending headache. "Then explain to me why the delegate from Pakistan would accuse your bloc?"

"Maybe to create discord? To weaken both our positions?" Elena replied. "It's a common strategy - divide and conquer."

Aarav's eyes bore into hers, searching for any hint of deceit. "And why should I believe you? Especially after today."

Elena stepped closer, her voice unwavering. "In the world of diplomacy, there's a principle: 'innocent until proven guilty.' You of all people should understand that."

He looked away, the weight of the day's events evident in his slouched posture. "If you were so sure that you weren't involved, then why didn't you confront him? Why didn't you defend yourself?"

Elena paused, considering her next words carefully. "Because the damage was already done. And because I hoped, foolishly perhaps, that you would trust me enough to come to me first."

Aarav's gaze snapped back to her, and for a moment, neither spoke. The distance between them felt much more than the few feet separating them.

"And why didn't you report it to the organizers if you truly believed it was part of my plan?" Elena continued, her voice softening.

Aarav hesitated, clearly taken aback. "Because… deep down, I didn't want to believe you were capable of something like that."

The atmosphere in the room shifted subtly. The animosity began to give way, replaced by a cautious understanding.

Elena let out a sigh of relief. "Thank you for at least giving me that benefit of the doubt. I just hope, in time, you'll see that I meant every word."

There was a knock on the door, breaking their intense exchange. Ritesh's voice filtered through, reminding them of the pending Mumbai exploration.

Elena turned towards the door, then looked back at Aarav. "Think about what I said. And maybe... just maybe, consider joining us tonight?"

With that, she left the room, leaving behind a contemplative Aarav, torn between his feelings and the events that had transpired.

The buzz of anticipation was palpable as the delegates milled around, boarding the bus for their Mumbai adventure. The sprawling metropolis, with its intoxicating blend of the ancient and the ultramodern, awaited them. From the narrow lanes of the old markets to the glittering skyline of the Bandra-Worli Sea Link, Mumbai had countless stories to offer.

Elena found a seat halfway down the bus, her eyes periodically darting towards the entrance. She had reserved the seat next to her with her bag, hoping against hope that Aarav would decide to come. She couldn't shake off the intensity of their conversation and felt a growing sense of unease as the minutes ticked by. Delegates filed in, laughing, chatting, the weight of the conference momentarily lifted. Yet, the seat next to Elena remained empty.

Back in the hotel room, Aarav was caught in two minds. Ritesh, ever the pragmatist, advised, "Look, mate, whether you believe her or not, you can't stay holed up here. It's Mumbai! And who knows, a change of scene might just give you the clarity you need."

After a few moments of contemplation, Aarav finally nodded, his decision made. Quickly slipping into a pair of jeans and a navy-blue hoodie, he made his way downstairs.

The bus engine roared to life just as Aarav approached, and for a moment, it seemed like he was too late. However, the driver spotted him and held on, allowing Aarav to board.

His entry caused a stir, whispers circulating about the intense committee session earlier that day. All eyes were on him, some curious, some sympathetic, and others judging. Trying to ignore the stares, Aarav's gaze locked onto Elena's. Their eyes met, and though words weren't exchanged, a thousand emotions were. With a hint of hesitancy, he moved towards the vacant seat next to her.

Elena, attempting to maintain her composure, shifted her bag to make room. "Thought you'd skip the tour," she remarked casually, though her relief was palpable.

Aarav, slipping into the seat, replied, "Almost did. But I've heard Mumbai is a city that can surprise you. Let's see if that's true."

The bus trundled on, and as the delegates were immersed in the sights and sounds of Mumbai, two of them embarked on a journey of their own – trying to navigate the delicate bridge between trust and doubt.

The atmosphere in the bus, already laden with whispered conversations and muffled laughter, was suddenly enriched by the gentle strains of music. Elena untangled her earphones and handed one to Aarav, a silent invitation to share a world that was, up until now, exclusively hers. The gesture was small, but in the chasm that had opened up between them, it was a bridge of sorts.

Their song selections took turns, a melodic conversation where words might fail. From Elena's fondness for Latin beats, which spoke of sultry nights and dancing shadows, to Aarav's preference for soulful Indian melodies that evoked rain-soaked streets and timeless tales of love. The music provided an escape from the simmering tensions, a reminder of simpler times and shared memories.

As the journey continued, the grandeur of Mumbai began to unfold. The bus meandered through the iconic Marine Drive, where the Arabian Sea playfully teased the city's boundaries. The long stretch was dotted with families, couples, and dreamers, all under the protective gaze of the Art Deco buildings, relics of a bygone era yet seamlessly woven into Mumbai's tapestry.

From there, the delegates were treated to the sight of the Gateway of India, standing tall and proud, a silent witness to the city's colonial past and its transition to a bustling metropolis. The nearby Taj Mahal Palace Hotel, with its majestic dome and intricate architecture, narrated tales of opulence, tragedies, and resilience.

The bus wove through the narrow lanes of Colaba, offering glimpses of Mumbai's multicultural heart. Antique stores nestled next to hipster cafes, and the scent of kebabs wafted through the air, mingling with the aroma of freshly baked pav, a local bread.

Their journey led them to the Worli Sea Face, where the Bandra-Worli Sea Link stood as a testament to modern engineering, bridging divides both geographical and metaphorical.

All along the way, Elena and Aarav found themselves lost, not just in the mesmerizing charm of Mumbai but also in the shared moments that the city serendipitously offered. Every now and then, their shoulders brushed, or their fingers nearly touched, and each time, it sent a frisson of electricity between them.

By the time the tour reached its final destination, the historic Chhatrapati Shivaji Maharaj Terminus with its gothic spires and stained-glass windows, the day had turned into twilight. The setting sun bathed the city in hues of gold and crimson, casting long shadows and illuminating dreams.

For Elena and Aarav, amidst the cacophony of Mumbai's heartbeat, in the gentle lull of shared songs, and the shared silences in between, something had shifted. They were still competitors, but Mumbai, with its myriad tales and timeless charm, had woven a new story for them, one that was only just beginning.

* * * * *

Mumbai Midnight Musings

The Mumbai tour had been an overwhelming sensory delight. As the bus began its journey back to the hotel, the accumulated exhaustion of the day finally caught up with the delegates. The vibrant chatter that had filled the air earlier had now mellowed down to soft murmurs and contemplative silences.

As the city's neon lights flitted past the window, Elena found herself lost in thought. The weight of Aarav's head on her shoulder was gentle, yet it held an undeniable gravity. With every bump and turn, she felt the warmth of his breath against her neck, stirring emotions she had never anticipated when she first walked into the conference.

Elena had always been pragmatic. She knew how fleeting MUN crushes could be. But this? This felt deeper. Every conversation, every shared smile, every stolen glance, seemed to echo in her mind, painting a tapestry of what could be. The question that gnawed at her was: Did Aarav feel the same?

She gently shifted in her seat to get a better look at his face. Even in slumber, Aarav looked intense, his brow slightly furrowed, as if he was solving an intricate puzzle in his dreams. Yet, there was a vulnerability to him that Elena hadn't noticed before.

She remembered the passion with which he had debated, the fierceness in his eyes when he had challenged her arguments. But now, this moment of quiet closeness painted a different picture. One of a boy who, beneath the layers of ambition and intelligence, was just searching for something more.

As the bus neared the hotel, the faint strains of a love song played on the radio, mirroring Elena's inner tumult. The lyrics spoke of unspoken emotions, of chances not taken, and the fragile line between love and friendship.

Suddenly, the bus jolted to a stop, rousing Aarav from his sleep. Disoriented, he looked around, quickly realizing his position and straightening up. Their eyes met, and for a heartbeat, everything seemed to pause. The weight of unspoken words and unresolved feelings hung thick in the air.

Clearing his throat, Aarav murmured, "Sorry about that. Long day."

Elena, her cheeks slightly flushed, replied with a playful smirk, "It's alright. But next time, maybe ask before using someone as a pillow?"

As they alighted from the bus, the tension between them was palpable. But beyond the uncertainty and the hesitations, there was a glimmer of something more profound, waiting to be explored.

* * * * *

Aarav's POV

Back in his room, Aarav sat down at the desk, the weight of numerous papers surrounding him. The resolution he was working on was vital, but his thoughts were elsewhere.

As he began to write, he found himself distracted by the lingering fragrance that wafted from his hoodie — Elena's perfume. Each time he caught its scent, images of their day together flooded his mind: the way her eyes lit up seeing the Gateway of India, her laughter ringing out as pigeons took flight around them at the Marine Drive, and the serene look on her face as they shared music.

He remembered the moment he had spotted the delicate earrings at a local shop. Intricately designed and shimmering under the warm Mumbai sun, they seemed to capture Elena's essence. A blend of strength, beauty, and complexity. Without a second thought, he'd purchased them, tucking them away in his pocket, hoping for the right moment to gift them.

Giving her the earrings tonight had been an impulse. Aarav wasn't sure if it was the magic of Mumbai, the intensity of the conference, or just the undeniable pull he felt towards Elena, but he wanted to give her something that symbolized their shared moments.

Pausing his work, Aarav leaned back in his chair, allowing himself to indulge in the memories of the day. The sensation of Elena's hair brushing against his cheek as they shared earphones, the sound of her voice as they discussed their favorite parts of Mumbai, and the warmth of her presence next to him in the bus.

But it wasn't just the day's memories that occupied his mind; it was also the heated debates, the passion with which Elena defended her stance, and the undeniable chemistry that sparked between them every time they locked eyes across the committee room. There was an energy, a current that flowed between them, and it was impossible to ignore.

Aarav shook his head, attempting to clear his thoughts. He needed to focus on the resolution. But as he dove into the intricacies of international law and diplomacy, a small smile played on his lips. Tomorrow was the final day of the conference, and while the tension between them was palpable, so was the anticipation.

For now, the pages before him demanded his attention. But as the night wore on, and the soft glow of Mumbai's lights streamed in through the window, Aarav knew that his story with Elena was just beginning.

Elena's POV

Elena sat on the balcony of her hotel room, the sounds of Mumbai's night-life serving as a distant serenade. The city that never slept was alive with energy, yet for her, the world had momentarily paused. Today had been a whirlwind — a blend of debates, unexpected confrontations, the magnetic charm of Mumbai, and the complex dance of emotions with Aarav.

She held the earrings up against the backdrop of the city lights. They were beautiful, and the gesture touched her deeply. It wasn't just the gift but the moment he chose to give it, the tender look in his eyes, the slight hesitation in his voice — all hinting at layers to Aarav that she was only beginning to unveil.

The day's adventures replayed in her mind. She recalled their shared music session on the bus, their playful banter as they explored the city, and the genuine curiosity in Aarav's eyes as he asked her about her life back in Mexico. But beyond all that, it was the unsaid feelings, the fleeting touches, and the shared glances that left the deepest imprint.

Her thoughts then drifted back to the conference. The intensity of their debates was undeniable. They were both passionate, driven, and fiercely protective of their country's stance. And yet, amid the heated exchanges, there were moments when she caught a softer, more vulnerable side of Aarav. The way his fingers would nervously tap against the table, the brief instances where his confident facade wavered — all revealing a young man battling his own insecurities.

Elena sighed. Tomorrow was the culmination of their efforts. While a part of her was geared up for the challenge, another part dreaded the inevitable farewell. Would they part as competitors? Friends? Or perhaps something more?

She leaned back, her gaze drifting to the stars. The universe had thrown them together in the most unexpected way. Two souls from different corners of the world, meeting at an international conference in the heart of Mumbai.

As she wrapped herself in her thoughts, there was a knock on her door. Shaking herself out of her reverie, she rose to answer it. But even before opening the door, a tiny voice inside her whispered, hoping it would be Aarav on the other side. The story between them was far from over, and Mumbai's starlit night still held many secrets.

* * * * *

Elena opened the door, her heart fluttering slightly as she found Aarav standing there, looking a touch unsure. "Hey," he started, rubbing the back of his neck. "I couldn't sleep, and I thought... maybe you'd like to grab something to eat? There's a great place in the hotel downstairs."

For a moment, Elena hesitated, the earlier intensity of their conversations playing in her mind. Then, remembering their shared moments and the softness she'd seen in him earlier, she nodded. "Sure, I could use some company."

They made their way to the hotel's terrace restaurant, which was dimly lit, casting a gentle glow over the tables. The soft strains of a sitar played in the background, creating a tranquil ambiance. They chose a secluded spot, and as they sat down, the city lights sparkled in the distance, a silent testament to Mumbai's vibrant spirit.

Looking over the menu, they both settled on pasta — a classic Aglio e Olio for Aarav and a creamy Alfredo for Elena. As they waited for their orders, an initial awkwardness settled between them. The day's events had thrown their dynamics off-kilter.

Yet, soon, the ice was broken when Aarav chuckled, "Never thought I'd be having pasta in Mumbai with a delegate from Mexico." Elena smiled, "Life has a way of surprising us."

As they spoke, the tension between them ebbed away. They shared stories from their childhood, their aspirations, dreams, and the quirks of their cultures. Elena laughed as Aarav tried to mimic a Mexican accent, while Aarav listened intently as Elena spoke about her family and the quaint streets of her hometown.

By the time their pasta arrived, they were engrossed in conversation, the plates merely a backdrop to their burgeoning bond. They debated over which dish was better, with Aarav playfully stealing a forkful from Elena's plate. Every so often, their hands would brush against each other, sending silent sparks flying.

It was near midnight, and the barriers between them were dissolving. It was evident that beneath the rivalry, a genuine fondness and perhaps the beginnings of something deeper were emerging.

"After paying the bill, they lingered on the terrace for a while longer, the cool Mumbai breeze caressing their faces. "You know," Elena began, looking at Aarav, "Today was a roller coaster, but I'm glad it ended this way."

Aarav nodded, his gaze intense, "Me too. Tomorrow's a new day, and who knows what it holds for us."

As they stood looking out at the city lights, Aarav reached into his pocket. "I got you something," he began hesitantly, pulling out a small velvet box. He opened it to reveal a pair of exquisite Indian earrings, the kind crafted with delicate filigree work and tiny pearl drops.

Elena's eyes widened in surprise. "Aarav... these are beautiful! When did you...?"

He looked away for a brief moment, seemingly gathering his thoughts. "When we were exploring the markets today," he began. "I saw you eyeing a similar pair. I wanted to get you something from India, something to remember this trip by."

She took the earrings from the box, admiring the intricate craftsmanship. "They're perfect," she whispered. "Thank you."

Aarav watched her, a small smile tugging at the corners of his lips. "I'm glad you like them. They'll look beautiful on you, especially with the Indian formal dress code for tomorrow."

A touch of pink graced Elena's cheeks as she looked up at him. "I'll wear them with pride," she replied softly.

For a moment, they stood there in silence, lost in the spell of the evening. The weight of what was transpiring between them, the uncertainty of the conference's outcome, and the sheer magnetism of the Mumbai night created a cocoon, holding them in its gentle embrace.

"I guess we should head back," Aarav finally said, breaking the silence.

Elena nodded, the reality of tomorrow's events suddenly looming large. "Yes, tomorrow is a big day."

The night sky above, sprinkled with stars, seemed to hold all the answers, and as they retreated to their rooms, the universe's whispers echoed with promises of new beginnings.

* * * * *

Chapter 6

THE FIRE WITHIN AND WITHOUT

The final day of the conference dawned with a golden hue, painting the Mumbai skyline with a burst of saffron and orange. As delegates prepared for the climactic culmination of the past few days, a palpable energy buzzed throughout the hotel.

Elena emerged from her room, looking resplendent in a royal blue kurti embroidered with intricate gold patterns. The delicate silver earrings Aarav had given her the previous night dangled gracefully from her ears, completing her ensemble. She paired the kurti with tailored cream-colored pants and gold strappy heels. Her hair was pulled back into a neat bun, a few tendrils framing her face, giving her an air of regal elegance.

A few foors down, Aarav stepped out, looking dashing in a white kurta paired with black pants. The kurta had a subtle sheen, adding a touch of sophistication to his look. His normally unruly hair was neatly combed, and his confident posture exuded a quiet strength.

As both walked towards the conference hall, they exchanged fleeting glances, silently acknowledging each other's presence without uttering a word. Their outfits, both traditional yet fitting for the MUN setting, set them apart, drawing many an appreciative gaze from fellow delegates.

After a sumptuous breakfast, where delegates from different countries shared their culinary delights, it was time to get down to business. Aarav and Elena, now settled into their respective roles and brimming with determination, made their way to their seats, folders and papers in tow.

The committee room was abuzz with chatter. Delegates were discussing strategies, forming alliances, and anticipating the day's proceedings. Whispers of the intense face-off between Aarav and Elena from the previous days were still making the rounds, adding an extra layer of anticipation.

The Chair called the session to order, and as the first delegate took to the podium, Aarav and Elena exchanged one last charged glance, each silently wishing the other luck while also preparing for the challenge that lay ahead. The final battle had begun.

The morning session commenced with delegates from various countries presenting their resolutions and proposed solutions to the committee's agenda. The room, bathed in soft, ambient light, was a haven of focused energy and intellectual fervor.

A representative from Japan began, suggesting technologically advanced sustainable solutions for environmental concerns. This was followed by Brazil highlighting the importance of preserving the Amazon rainforest and their strategies to combat illegal logging.

Elena, leading the 'Sustainable Development' bloc, proved her mettle by steering the discussions in a direction that favored her bloc's interests. Every time a delegate presented a solution that didn't align with her bloc's vision, Elena was quick to diplomatically point out potential loopholes or areas of improvement. She did this not by belittling others, but by building on their ideas, showcasing her collaborative spirit.

Aarav, on the other hand, showed masterful skill in rallying support for the 'Right to Development' bloc. His approach was grounded in the socio-economic realities of developing countries. With every point raised against his bloc, he countered with data, quoting studies and international conventions, always emphasizing the need for a balanced approach.

Throughout the session, both Aarav and Elena exhibited their profound understanding of the subject. They skillfully navigated through complex issues, building on arguments and, at times, even conceding to points that made sense.

What was interesting to the onlookers was the unspoken understanding between the two. It was clear they respected each other's perspectives. When Aarav made a compelling point, Elena would nod in acknowledgment, and vice versa. Their debates, though heated, never crossed the boundary of mutual respect.

Lunchtime neared, and the committee took a break. Delegates spilled out of the room, discussing the morning's proceedings, forming new alliances, and re-strategizing. The morning had set the stage for what promised to be an explosive afternoon session, where final resolutions would be debated and voted upon.

The lunch hall buzzed with the energetic discussions of the delegates. Elena and Aarav found a relatively quieter corner to discuss the strategy for the upcoming session. Just as they started discussing the implications of China's proposed amendments, a loud ruckus interrupted their conversation.

Both of them turned to see the delegate of Pakistan in a heated argument with the delegate from Israel. Words escalated quickly and, before anyone could intervene, a water jug was accidentally knocked over. The water streamed across the table, pooling around several electronic devices. There was a moment of stunned silence before a sharp hissing sound was heard, followed by sparks flying from a delegate's laptop. In seconds, a small fire started, its flames quickly growing, licking up the papers strewn across the table.

Immediate panic ensued. Delegates jumped from their seats, some trying to stomp out the fire, others rushing to save their important documents. A few quick-thinking individuals grabbed fire extinguishers and aimed them at the blaze. Smoke began filling the hall, triggering the fire alarms. The piercing sound added to the chaos.

The organizing committee and the Executive Board were quick to respond. The president of the committee, a stern figure known for his discipline, stood up and shouted over the din, "Evacuate immediately! Follow the fire exit signs and gather at the designated assembly point!"

The delegates, shaken and alarmed, began to move rapidly, leaving behind their belongings. Elena grabbed Aarav's arm, ensuring they stayed together amidst the confusion. As they made their way to the nearest exit, they could see hotel staff rushing in to manage the situation.

Outside, as they stood at the assembly point, emergency sirens wailed in the distance. Elena looked around to ensure that all members of her bloc were accounted for. Aarav, meanwhile, was engaged in a discussion with a few senior members about the incident.

"It was an accident, but it could have catastrophic implications for the conference," he said, concern evident in his voice.

Elena approached him, "We need to regroup and ensure everyone is safe. We'll deal with the conference logistics later."

Their conversation was cut short by the president's announcement. "Given the situation, all delegates are instructed to return to their rooms and await further information. The hotel staff will handle the situation, and we'll keep you updated."

Back in their rooms, the gravity of the situation began to sink in for Elena and Aarav. Such incidents were rare, and the ramifications could be severe. They knew the rest of the day would be challenging, both in managing the aftermath of the fire and in steering the conference back on track.

An hour of tension and uncertainty passed before the notification chimed on Elena and Aarav's phones simultaneously. They both checked, finding an official message from the MUN organizers:

"Dear Delegates,

We are relieved to inform you that the situation has been managed and the area deemed safe. We deeply regret to inform you that due to the unforeseen circumstances, the remaining committee sessions for the day have been rescheduled to commence tomorrow morning.

Furthermore, after a preliminary investigation, the delegate of Pakistan has been suspended from the conference, effective immediately, due to a breach of the code of conduct.

We understand this disrupts the planned flow of discussions and deliberations, but we prioritize your safety above all else. Kindly use this time to refine your positions and re-strategize for the extended conference day tomorrow. We appreciate your understanding and cooperation.

Warm regards,

The Organizing Committee."

Elena read the message out loud the message from the OC to Isabella, her roommate, who had just returned from the assembly point. "I can't believe it escalated to this," Isabella remarked, clearly shaken.

"I know," Elena replied, running a hand through her hair. "And it all happened so quickly."

Elsewhere, Aarav was in his room with Ritesh. Ritesh exhaled, leaning back against the wall. "Man, that was crazy. Though I did anticipate some fireworks in this MUN, I never imagined they'd be literal."

Aarav smirked, despite the situation. "Well, it gives us some time to recalibrate our strategy. With the delegate of Pakistan gone, there'll be a shift in alliances and dynamics."

Back in Elena's room, she was lost in thought, the recent events still fresh in her mind. "This suspension will tilt the balance," she mused, "Pakistan was a significant voice in the sustainable bloc."

"Yes," Isabella replied, "And with tomorrow being the last day, it's going to be one intense finale."

As evening set in, the delegates made the most of their unexpected free time. Some gathered in the lobby to discuss the day's shocking events, while others retreated to their rooms to refine their resolutions. Elena and Aarav, each in their respective rooms, found themselves reviewing their stances, preparing for the final showdown, and anticipating the challenges and opportunities that the next day would bring.

Elena stared at her phone for a few minutes, her fingers hovering over the keyboard, wondering if it was a good idea. Then, taking a deep breath, she typed, "Hey, want to hang out this evening? Maybe grab a coffee or something?"

She pressed send and waited.

Aarav, on the other end, was taken aback when he saw the message. He paused, then quickly typed, "Yeah, sure. Sounds good. Where?"

Elena replied, "There's a small café two blocks from here. I've heard they serve some good local desserts."

"Sounds tempting. See you in 20?"

"Perfect," Elena typed back, her heart fluttering slightly. She quickly changed into a comfortable pair of jeans and a soft white top, and threw on a lightweight scarf for good measure.

Meanwhile, Aarav chose a pair of black jeans and a casual blue shirt. He brushed his hair, giving himself one last look in the mirror before heading out.

They met in the hotel lobby. Elena's eyes caught Aarav's as they approached each other. There was a brief, charged silence before Aarav said, "You look nice."

Elena smiled, "You too. Let's head out?"

Aarav couldn't help but observe the subtle changes in Elena's appearance since the first day of the conference. Her hair, usually tied back for the formal sessions, cascaded in gentle waves down her shoulders. He noticed the faint aroma of jasmine as she walked past him, a scent that reminded him of the gardens in his childhood home.

Elena, on the other hand, was equally observant. The relaxed version of Aarav was a contrast to the fierce debater she had come to know in the committee. The way his shirt was slightly crumpled at the edges, the casual ease with which he carried himself, it was refreshing and, in a way, endearing.

They began their walk to a nearby café. The bustling streets of Mumbai enveloped them, with colorful stalls selling trinkets, the aromas of various local delicacies filling the air, and the soft murmurs of evening conversations.

As they navigated through the lanes, Elena initiated the conversation, "You know, I've always been fascinated by Mumbai. The blend of cultures, the history..."

Aarav chimed in, "Yeah, it's a city that never sleeps. There's always something happening. The vibrancy, the spirit... it's unmatched. Have you been to India before?"

Elena shook her head, "No, this is my first time. But I've read a lot about it. The architecture, the festivals... I wish I had more time to explore."

They reached the café and took a seat by the window. Aarav ordered two coffees and some local snacks. As they waited for their order, Elena hesitated for a moment before asking, "Aarav, why did you choose to represent India in the MUN? I mean, besides the fact that you're from here."

Aarav took a moment before answering, "Well, for one, I've always felt a deep connection to my country's history and culture. But more than that, it's about representing a perspective, a voice that often gets overshadowed in global forums."

Elena nodded, appreciating his passion. "It's amazing how deeply you feel about it. For me, Mexico is home, it's where I grew up. But I've always been curious about the world. And MUNs give me that opportunity to understand and engage."

The conversation drifted from personal experiences to shared ambitions. Elena spoke about her love for poetry and how she secretly hoped to publish a book someday. Aarav confessed his aspiration to enter Indian diplomacy, to make a difference on a larger scale.

The hours seemed to fly by. The evening transformed into a blend of laughter, shared stories, and an unspoken comfort. The fierce competitors from the conference room were now two young souls connecting over dreams and hopes.

As they left the café, the city lights reflecting in their eyes, there was an unsaid promise to cherish this newfound bond, irrespective of the challenges the next day's sessions would bring.

* * * * *

The Thin Line: Between Protocol and Passion

The hotel's facade, illuminated in soft amber lights, seemed to draw them closer as they approached the entrance. They exchanged light banter, the energy from their deep conversation at the café still very palpable between them.

As they stepped into the opulent lobby, the elevator's mirrored doors slid open. They entered, Aarav pressing the button for their floor. The elevator started its ascent, and the reflective walls displayed their reflections back to them — two individuals, so different yet so connected.

In the quiet hum of the elevator, with the city's distant sounds muffled, Elena caught Aarav's gaze. Those eyes, which earlier in the day had fired arguments with conviction and passion, now seemed vulnerable, sincere. Aarav, reading the same depth of emotion in Elena's eyes, felt a magnetic pull.

He took a hesitant step closer, the gap between them decreasing with each heartbeat. Then, in a moment, as if guided by the same impulse, Aarav leaned in, capturing Elena's lips with his own.

Time seemed to stand still. The world outside the elevator ceased to exist, and all that mattered was the electric charge between them. The kiss was gentle, yet full of unsaid emotions — a blend of their day's exhilaration, the chemistry they felt, and the anticipation of the days to come.

The soft chime of the elevator reaching their floor startled them back into reality. They pulled apart, their eyes wide with surprise at their own impulsiveness. There was a brief moment of awkwardness before Elena, ever the diplomat, said with a sly smile, "Well, that was... unexpected."

Aarav chuckled, a tad sheepishly, "Yes, it was. But not entirely unwelcome, I hope?"

Elena, her eyes sparkling, replied, "Definitely not unwelcome."

As they exited the elevator, the palpable tension between them made way for a comfortable silence. They walked to their respective rooms, both lost in the whirlwind of emotions from the evening. Before parting, Aarav softly said, "Good night, Elena."

"Good night, Aarav," she replied, the hint of a smile playing on her lips.

As the doors closed behind them, they both knew that the upcoming day would be a test of their newfound connection. But for now, they basked in the afterglow of an unexpected moment, one that promised more possibilities.

Elena entered her room, her fingers still tingling from the brief touch of Aarav's lips. The room, bathed in the soft hue of the bedside lamp, seemed almost otherworldly after the intensity of the evening. She let out a deep sigh, sinking into the plush chair by the window.

What just happened? she pondered. The MUN was supposed to be about debating, winning arguments, making alliances, not this... this whirlwind of emotions. She had always prided herself on her ability to stay focused, to keep her personal feelings separate from her professional demeanor. And yet, Aarav had effortlessly breached those barriers.

She recalled the first time they locked horns in the committee, the fire in his eyes, the passion in his voice. *Was it the thrill of the challenge that drew me to him? Or was it something deeper?*

Elena shook her head, trying to dismiss the torrent of emotions. But there was no denying it; she was smitten. Not just by his good looks or his debating skills but by the man behind those fierce arguments. The thoughtful Aarav, who listened to music that spoke of ancient Indian tales, who cared deeply about his nation and the world.

But it's complicated, she admitted to herself. Their professional rivalry, their personal histories, the uncharted waters of their blossoming relationship; it was a delicate dance. Elena was no stranger to heartbreak, and the last thing she wanted was to end up with regrets.

* * * * *

On the other side of the hotel corridor, Aarav sat at his desk, the screen of his laptop casting a soft glow. But the words and data on the screen made no sense to him. His thoughts were consumed by Elena, by the electric moment they had shared.

Why did I do that? he chided himself. The logical part of his brain, the part that always formulated arguments and strategies, reprimanded him for acting on impulse. But another part, a deeper, more primal part, was rejoicing.

He remembered the way her eyes had widened in surprise, the softness of her lips, the hint of vulnerability. It was intoxicating. Aarav had always been the master of his emotions, never letting personal feelings cloud his judgment. But with Elena, all bets were off.

He leaned back, rubbing his temples, trying to make sense of the tumult within. He admired Elena, respected her, and now, undeniably, was drawn to her. But with the MUN's intensity and their roles as opponents, was it wise to pursue this?

Ugh! Aarav groaned, *Life would be so much simpler if emotions came with a playbook.*

The night deepened, and as the hotel settled into quietude, two souls grappled with their feelings, each hoping for clarity by dawn.

* * * * *

THE TENSION OF UNITY

The morning sun filtered through the tall windows of the hotel's dining area, casting a golden hue over everything. Delegates bustled around, chatting animatedly about the final day of the conference. The atmosphere was electric, with the anticipation of the climax of days of intense debate.

As Elena made her way to the breakfast spread, she couldn't help but glance in Aarav's direction. Their eyes met, and there was an unmistakable spark. It was a look that held promises, secrets, and questions all at once.

Walking over to him, she discreetly handed Aarav a small, intricately designed pin. "Thought this might go with your suit," she whispered.

Aarav looked at the pin, a beautiful blend of traditional Indian design with modern flair. "Thank you," he replied, his voice soft. There was so much he wanted to say, but the words seemed to be stuck. He affixed the pin to his suit, feeling its weight, both literal and metaphorical.

Breakfast continued in a whirl of conversations, but the two of them were acutely aware of each other's presence. Every now and then, their eyes would meet, exchanging silent words.

As breakfast concluded, the delegates began to make their way to the committee room. The chatter was a mix of excitement for the final session and speculations about yesterday's incident involving the delegate of Pakistan. The committee room was abuzz, with whispers and last-minute negotiations.

Elena and Aarav found themselves on opposite sides of the room, each heading their respective blocs. The day's proceedings were crucial, and while the previous day's personal revelations had altered the dynamics between them, they both knew they had a duty to their blocs and their countries. The chairperson tapped the gavel, signaling the start of the session.

The chairperson's gavel cut through the chatter like a knife, bringing everyone's attention to the front. Aarav took a deep breath, standing up with a confident yet composed demeanor.

"Respected Chair, honorable delegates," he began, "I propose an unmoderated caucus for fifteen minutes."

There were murmurs around the room. Unmods were standard, but this early into the session was a bit unexpected. The chair considered the proposal and put it to a vote. The majority of the hands shot up in favor.

During the unmod, delegates milled about, discussing their viewpoints and strategies. Aarav approached Elena, signaling for her to join him in a corner of the room.

"Elena," Aarav began, his tone serious yet hopeful, "I've been thinking. Instead of us presenting divided fronts, how about we merge our blocs? We can draft a unified resolution, combining the strengths of both our arguments. This way, we ensure that the developed countries support the developing nations in a manner beneficial to both."

Elena raised an eyebrow, intrigued. "Go on."

Aarav continued, "We can reference international legal principles, such as the Common But Differentiated Responsibilities (CBDR) under the UN Framework Convention on Climate Change. It emphasizes the shared obligation of all nations in environmental protection but acknowledges that developed countries have a greater historical responsibility and therefore, a heightened duty to assist."

Elena nodded, clearly engaged. "We can also bring in the International Covenant on Economic, Social, and Cultural Rights. It emphasizes the duty of States to ensure the rights of everyone, including the most marginalized."

Aarav's eyes lit up, "Exactly! Additionally, recent reports by the World Bank and the UNDP highlight the advantages of international cooperation, especially in sustainable development. The synergy can result in exponential growth and progress, benefiting all involved."

Elena paused for a moment, considering. "While I see the potential advantages, how do we ensure the concerns of our respective blocs are equally represented and not overshadowed?"

Aarav replied, "Through meticulous drafting and careful compromise. We can also include mechanisms to ensure periodic review and adjustment, based on the evolving needs of member states."

Elena smiled, "You've really thought this through, haven't you?"

Aarav chuckled, "It's what we do, isn't it? Think, strategize, and hopefully, make a difference."

Elena extended her hand, "Alright, let's do this."

Aarav shook her hand firmly, "Together."

The fifteen minutes seemed to fly by. As the unmod came to an end and the delegates returned to their seats, there was an air of palpable excitement. Two of the strongest blocs, previously in contention, were now on the verge of presenting a joint front. The rest of the day promised to be nothing short of historic.

Aarav and Elena walked towards their respective blocs, their purposeful strides exuding a newfound unity. The delegates could sense the palpable change in dynamics, the atmosphere charged with cautious optimism.

Elena's Bloc:

Elena, always the eloquent speaker, started, "My esteemed delegates, we've always stood for sustainable development, emphasizing the need for developed countries to take their historical responsibilities seriously. While we have made compelling arguments, we have also met formidable resistance."

She continued, "In light of recent events and after considerable discussion with Delegate of India, we have an opportunity. An opportunity to merge our blocs, to craft a resolution that balances the rights and duties of all countries, upholding international law and principles."

Delegate from Brazil asked, "How do we ensure that our concerns aren't overshadowed?"

Elena replied, "By being part of the drafting process. By ensuring our voices, concerns, and suggestions are embedded into the resolution. The principles of CBDR and international covenants act as our backbone. It's a chance for historic collaboration."

Delegate from South Africa added, "But what about accountability and transparency?"

Elena smiled, "That's the beauty of it. We incorporate mechanisms for regular reviews, updates, and checks. Everyone is held accountable."

The bloc murmured in agreement, the idea gaining traction.

Aarav's Bloc:

Meanwhile, Aarav was making his pitch. "Delegates, we've always emphasized self-reliance and the autonomy of sovereign nations. But collaboration doesn't mean compromising sovereignty. By working with Elena's bloc, we can usher in a new era of cooperation."

The Delegate from Japan interjected, "But how do we ensure that our funds and technologies don't get misused?"

Aarav responded, "Through stringent guidelines, checks, and balances. We're not proposing a one-size-fits-all solution. Rather, a dynamic and adaptable framework that can be tailored to individual countries' needs, all the while adhering to international norms."

The Delegate from Germany added, "So, it's a give and take?"

Aarav nodded, "Exactly. In this globalized world, interdependence is inevitable. We strengthen our ties, benefit from shared resources, and grow together."

There was a pause as the bloc members contemplated. Then the Delegate from Australia said, "Alright, we trust you, India. Let's give this a shot."

As the two blocs formally merged, the committee room buzzed with whispers and exchanged glances. The unexpected unity between two powerhouse blocs caught everyone's attention. The alliance of Aarav and Elena had not only shifted the power dynamics of the committee but also charted a new path of diplomacy, setting the stage for an intense and intriguing culmination.

The expanded resolution, drawing upon the vast intricacies of international climate diplomacy and the multifaceted issues within the UNFCCC, was as follows:

DRAFT RESOLUTION 1.1

Topic: Strengthening Global Collaboration for Climate Action within the framework of UNFCCC

The UNFCCC,

Acknowledging the historical and disproportionate contributions to global greenhouse gas emissions by developed nations,

Reaffirming the commitments made under the Paris Agreement, with a particular focus on the target to keep global temperature rise this century well below 2 degrees Celsius above pre-industrial levels,

Recognizing the principle of Common But Differentiated Responsibilities and Respective Capabilities (CBDR-RC) as a fundamental cornerstone of international climate change negotiations,

Cognizant of the urgent need for scaled-up climate finance, technology transfer, and capacity-building for the Global South,

1. *Urges* developed countries to review and scale up their Nationally Determined Contributions (NDCs) by 2025, striving for carbon neutrality by 2050.
2. *Mandates* the creation of a High-Level Panel on Climate Finance, to ensure the goal of mobilizing $100 billion annually by 2025 is not just met but surpassed, emphasizing the importance of grant-based resources for adaptation.
3. *Calls upon* the operationalization of the Warsaw International Mechanism for Loss and Damage, to comprehensively address non-economic losses and incorporate climate migration challenges.
4. *Recommends* a Global Climate Technology Blueprint under the Climate Technology Centre and Network (CTCN), tailored to address the specific needs and challenges of developing countries, ensuring not only transfer but also indigenous development of technologies.

5. *Advocates* for a "Climate Knowledge Exchange Program" - a rigorous, globally interconnected program promoting the sharing of scientific research, best practices, and innovative policies among nations.
6. *Stresses* the need for the Integration of Gender and Climate Change strategy, ensuring women, often the most vulnerable to climate impacts, are at the forefront of climate action and decision-making.
7. *Proposes* the establishment of a 'Vulnerability Index' which takes into account sea-level rise, desertification, and climate-induced socioeconomic challenges to guide climate finance allocation.
8. *Promotes* the strengthening of the Climate Action Enhancement Package (CAEP) to fast-track NDC enhancement for willing countries.

Aarav, meticulously addressing the committee, said, "This resolution is not just another document. It represents the aspirations of billions who bear the brunt of our past mistakes. It's a testament to our capacity, as global actors, to envision a resilient, equitable future."

Elena admired Aarav's ability to weave intricate policy matters with the human aspect of climate change. His speech was not just about international laws and conventions but also about real lives, aspirations, and global justice. It was this blend of expertise and empathy that set Aarav apart.

The committee room was filled with an air of cautious optimism. The journey ahead was complex, but with leaders like Aarav and Elena at the forefront, there was hope for genuine, transformative change.

The room, which had been filled with a sense of unity and cautious optimism, was suddenly thick with tension as the delegate of China confidently stood up, placing a new draft resolution on the table. This move wasn't entirely unexpected. China, with its vast manufacturing capacities and economic interests, had often been a focal point of such discussions. However, the timing was impeccable, strategically placing it just before the break to let the content simmer in the minds of the delegates.

DRAFT RESOLUTION 2.1

Topic: Realistic and Pragmatic Approach to Climate Action within the framework of UNFCCC

The UNFCCC,

Recalling the socio-economic development rights of every nation,

Emphasizing the principle of equitable distribution of the global carbon space,

Affirming the commitment to addressing climate change while ensuring the right to development,

1. **Encourages** nations to transition to cleaner technologies while respecting their unique developmental timelines and national circumstances.
2. **Suggests** the establishment of an International Carbon Market, allowing countries to trade in carbon credits, promoting cleaner technologies

while ensuring no compromise on economic growth.

3. **Calls for** enhanced South-South cooperation, with nations sharing best practices, technological solutions, and innovative policy measures suitable for their unique challenges.
4. **Requests** developed countries to consider the historic carbon debt and facilitate technology transfer without attaching conditionalities.
5. **Urges** a re-evaluation of the definition of 'developed' and 'developing' nations, keeping in mind the dynamic nature of global economic realities.
6. **Promotes** the concept of 'Climate-Adjusted GDP' to bring a more realistic perspective to national contributions to global climate action.

The delegate of China, with a calm demeanor, began, "This resolution does not undermine the urgency of climate action. Instead, it offers a pragmatic approach, respecting the varied developmental trajectories of nations. The world cannot be handcuffed by unrealistic expectations, stunting growth and development."

Whispers broke out across the room. Many delegates, especially from developing nations, found themselves torn between the two resolutions. Both offered sound arguments, yet their core philosophies seemed at odds.

Elena exchanged a quick, concerned glance with Aarav. They both realized that the day ahead was going to be more challenging than they had anticipated. The foundation they had laid was now being tested, and the game of diplomacy and negotiation had truly begun.

The ringing of the gavel signaled the start of the break, but neither Elena nor Aarav had the luxury to rest. They understood that the next hour would determine the fate of their resolution. Committee breaks, often mistaken for a time of leisure, were the most crucial for diplomacy and lobbying in the Model UN circuit.

Elena quickly gathered her bloc, forming a tight circle in one corner of the room. They needed to be united in their approach and message. While she handled the smaller nations, she signaled Aarav to approach the bigger players. Elena's voice was firm, "We've come this far. Let's stay strong and coherent. Highlight the key benefits of our resolution. Remember, this isn't just about today; it's about a sustainable future."

On the other side, Aarav found himself face to face with the delegates from Russia, Brazil, and South Africa. "Our resolution," he began calmly, "understands the balance between development and environmental concerns. China's draft, while commendable, puts too much emphasis on industrial growth without addressing the imminent environmental consequences. We can't afford a half measure now."

As he spoke, Aarav used various tactics, from appealing to a nation's global image to the nitty-gritty details of their own national policies, showing how their resolution was better aligned with their interests.

Elena, meanwhile, engaged with delegates from African nations, highlighting the funding, technology transfer, and capacity-building opportunities that their resolution offered. She emphasized, "Our proposal ensures that the developed nations not only pledge but are held accountable for their commitments. This isn't just about the environment; it's about justice."

The atmosphere in the room was tense. Every delegate was engaged in fervent conversation, some nodding in agreement while others gestured animatedly, debating the fine points. The room was alive with the buzz of diplomacy.

Outside the committee room, Aarav caught up with Elena for a brief moment. Both were exhausted but determined. "How's it looking?" he asked.

"Uncertain," Elena admitted. "But we've put in our best. Let's hope for the best."

Aarav nodded, "No matter what happens next, remember we've made a difference."

Their shared vision, not just for victory but for global good, was evident in their determination. As they re-entered the committee room, they knew that the final battle of diplomacy awaited.

The delegates returned to the committee room, the air heavy with anticipation. The chairs, recognizing the gravity of the situation, maintained a strict decorum.

The Chairperson addressed the assembly, "Delegates, we will now move to the introduction of the draft resolution by the delegations of India and Mexico. You may proceed."

Elena and Aarav stood up. They had strategized about this moment during the break. Elena began, her voice echoing in the silent hall, "Honorable Chair, distinguished delegates, we present before you a resolution that embodies the spirit of cooperation and mutual growth. A resolution that does not merely provide a roadmap but paves the path towards sustainable development."

Aarav took over smoothly, laying out the specifics. "This resolution stresses on technology transfer, capacity building in developing countries, and more importantly, transparent and accountable financial mechanisms. Developed countries need to honor their commitments not just in letter but in spirit."

With the introduction complete, the Chair opened the floor to Points of Information.

The delegate of China, known for his razor-sharp arguments, was quick to stand. "While we appreciate the spirit of the resolution presented by India and Mexico, how does the delegation propose to ensure that developing countries do not misuse the funds and technologies, given the lack of stringent checks and balances in their systems?"

Elena was prepared. "Thank you for the question. Our resolution proposes the creation of an international oversight committee under the UNFCCC. This committee will not only monitor the allocation and use of funds but will also ensure that technology transfers are used for their intended purpose."

China's ally, the delegate from Iran, questioned further, "The resolution mentions a 'flexible mechanism' for developed nations to meet their financial commitments. How can we trust such vagueness, especially when historically, many promises have been broken?"

Aarav replied, "The flexible mechanism isn't a loophole but an acknowledgment of economic realities. Every developed nation might not have the same financial capabilities at all times. The mechanism ensures they still contribute in terms of technology or expertise when direct financial aid is difficult."

The room was on fire with sharp questions and sharper answers. The bloc led by China wasn't going to make it easy. Every clause of the resolution was scrutinized, every intention questioned.

During a particularly intense round of questioning, Aarav leaned over to Elena and whispered, "Stay strong. We've got this." She nodded, steeling herself for the next round of points.

It was clear that this was not just a battle of policies but a clash of ideologies and visions for the future. The session was shaping up to be one of the most memorable in the history of MUN conferences.

The delegate from Russia, a key ally of China, stood up with a sly grin. "I would like to direct this question to the delegate of India. How can we trust India's intentions in pushing for this resolution when historically, the country has been known to prioritize its own economic growth over global environmental concerns?"

The room fell silent, awaiting Aarav's response. Elena glanced at him, worriedly. This was a direct attack, not on the resolution, but on India's credibility.

Aarav, however, seemed unfazed. Standing up, he cleared his throat and began, "Thank you for your question, delegate of Russia. It's essential to understand the context and nuances of a nation's actions rather than making sweeping generalizations."

He continued, “India, like any other sovereign nation, has the primary responsibility of ensuring the well-being and prosperity of its people. Economic growth has been a means to lift millions out of poverty. But that doesn’t mean we’ve turned a blind eye to environmental concerns.”

Pointing to a chart, Aarav elaborated, “In the past decade, India has made significant strides in renewable energy, becoming one of the world leaders in solar energy. The International Solar Alliance, initiated by India, is a testament to our commitment to green energy. We’ve pledged to increase the non-fossil fuel share of our energy capacity to 40% by 2030.”

Not letting up, Aarav added, “Furthermore, our recent policies, like the ban on single-use plastics, massive tree plantation drives, and stringent vehicular emission norms, showcase our dedication to a sustainable future. Our intentions, delegate of Russia, are clear in our actions.”

Russia’s delegate seemed momentarily stunned by Aarav’s articulate and well-researched rebuttal. Whispers filled the room, and nods of agreement were visible among many delegates.

Elena leaned in, whispering, “Brilliantly handled, Aarav.”

Aarav, his face flushed from the exchange, whispered back, “We’ve come too far to let baseless allegations derail our efforts. We’ve got a planet to save.”

The atmosphere in the committee room was charged. Every delegate knew that this wasn’t just a competition anymore. The stakes were real, and the future was on the line.

The intense discussions and heated debates finally gave way to the moment everyone had been waiting for: the voting on the resolutions.

"Delegates," the chair began, "we will now move into voting procedures. We have two draft resolutions on the floor. According to UNA-USA procedures, each resolution will be voted on separately, starting with the one introduced by the delegate of India and Mexico."

Elena and Aarav exchanged a nervous glance. The future of their resolution rested in the hands of their fellow delegates.

"Before we move into voting, are there any motions on the floor?" the chair inquired.

Silence.

"Very well," the chair continued. "We will now vote on the draft resolution presented by India and Mexico. All in favor, please raise your placards high."

A sea of placards went up. Elena and Aarav tried to count, but the tension was palpable, and numbers seemed to blur.

"All against?"

A significant number of placards rose in opposition, primarily driven by the bloc led by China.

"All abstaining?"

A few more placards went up.

The chairperson, flanked by two assistants, began tallying the votes. The room was on edge, the silence only broken by the occasional shuffle of papers.

After what felt like an eternity, the chairperson announced, "The resolution has passed in the first round with a majority, but not a two-thirds majority. We will now move to a second round of voting."

The second round saw a similar pattern. The resolution was close, but still shy of the required two-thirds majority.

The weight of the moment pressed on Elena and Aarav as the third round of voting commenced. This was their last chance.

Again, placards went up in succession—favor, against, abstain. The tallies were quickly done this time.

The chairperson took a moment, looking at the numbers, then announced, "By a slim majority in the third round, the draft resolution presented by India and Mexico has passed."

A wave of relief washed over Elena and Aarav. They exchanged triumphant smiles, their hard work and collaboration finally bearing fruit.

The room erupted into a mixture of applause and hushed conversations. While some were elated, others, notably the Chinese bloc, looked on with disappointment.

Yet, for Elena and Aarav, it was a moment of validation, a testament to their dedication, diplomacy, and the strength of their resolution. The world, as represented by their fellow delegates, had placed its faith in their vision for a sustainable future.

As the applause dwindled and the conference room began to empty, the Chairperson called attention to the next item on the agenda: the feedback session.

* * * * *

CONFESSIONS AND CONCLUSIONS

"All delegates, please be seated. We will now transition to the feedback session, where the Executive Board (EB) will provide insights into the committee's performance over the past few days."

A palpable mix of exhaustion, pride, and anticipation hung in the air. For many, this was a chance to learn, to grow, and to prepare for the next Model UN conference.

Elena and Aarav, having successfully navigated a turbulent committee session, were particularly interested in what the EB had to say. They took seats next to each other, silently exchanging glances as the Chairperson began.

The Chairperson, Ms. Patel, a seasoned MUNer with years of experience both as a delegate and as a member of the Executive Board, started, "Firstly, I want to congratulate every single delegate here. The past few days have seen rigorous debate, challenging diplomacy, and commendable collaboration."

She then shifted her focus to the draft resolutions, "Both the resolutions that came to the floor today were impressive. They showcased deep understanding, thorough research, and innovative solutions. The resolution from the India-Mexico bloc, in particular, managed to garner a lot of support, despite facing fierce competition. Aarav, Elena, well done."

Elena beamed, and Aarav nodded in acknowledgment.

The Vice-Chair, Mr. Hassan, took over, "I'd like to address the importance of decorum and adherence to protocol. While most of you were exemplary, we did have a few instances that deviated from expected standards." His gaze turned momentarily stern, likely referring to the incident with the delegate of Pakistan. "In the future, always remember the significance and gravity of this platform."

Ms. Patel chimed in again, "But overall, the level of debate, the quality of questions, and the spirited discussions were commendable. Each of you brought something unique to the table, and it was a privilege to witness the making of future diplomats and world leaders."

Aarav, feeling the weight of the past few days, whispered to Elena, "It's over. We did it."

Elena nodded, "We did, but this is just the beginning."

The feedback session concluded with individual comments for delegates who wished for specific feedback. As the room gradually emptied, there was a tangible sense of achievement, camaraderie, and the bittersweet end of yet another Model UN conference.

The EB's feedback session continued as delegates eagerly waited for insights on their performance. Ms. Patel shuffled her papers, and then focused on the delegate of China's resolution.

"While we're on the topic of resolutions," she began, her tone even but assertive, "I'd like to address the draft presented by the delegate of China and his allies. It's crucial that we understand why it wasn't considered for final voting."

There was a hushed murmur in the room. China's resolution, though exhaustive and detailed, had taken many by surprise, and several delegates were curious about its rejection.

Mr. Hassan took the lead, "The resolution presented by the delegate of China had a significant oversight in one of its clauses. It failed to consider a crucial tenet of the UNFCCC. While the idea was commendable, the resolution's wording and structure were not in line with the current accepted practices. It would have potentially led to conflicts with existing agreements."

Ms. Patel added, "Furthermore, the presentation of the resolution so late in the conference hindered its chances considerably. Proper time management ensures everyone has a fair chance to debate, deliberate, and come to a consensus. It's not just about presenting a resolution; it's about allowing the committee adequate time to understand and dissect it. Unfortunately, this was a misstep on the part of the delegate of China."

A few nods of agreement rippled through the room, and the delegate of China, though visibly disappointed, nodded in acknowledgment. It was a hard lesson, but a necessary one in the world of diplomacy and debate.

Elena leaned over to Aarav, "It was a close call. China's resolution had some strong points."

Aarav whispered back, "True, but in MUN, it's not just about what you say, but also how and when you say it. Time management and understanding of protocols are just as critical as the content."

She nodded, appreciating the depth of the learning experience this conference had provided. The two of them, along with all the other delegates, had witnessed firsthand the importance of every detail when it came to international diplomacy.

Delegates had taken off their blazers, loosened their ties, and there was a buzz of chatter as everyone waited for the next segment: Motion of Entertainment.

Ms. Patel, with a mischievous grin, addressed the committee, "Delegates, I know the past few days have been intense, and you've all worked extremely hard. But now, it's time for some fun. We've collected confession chits throughout the conference, and we'll be reading them out. Please note that these are anonymous and meant in good humor."

Mr. Hassan, having picked up the first chit, read, "To the delegate of France, your passion for environmental policies is only rivaled by how passionately you sip your coffee. #EcoFriendlyCrush."

There was a round of chuckles and the delegate of France blushed slightly, taking a playful bow.

Ms. Patel continued with another chit, "To the delegate of Russia, your stern expressions during debates are secretly adored by someone here. #RussianRomance."

This caused a lot more laughter, and the delegate of Russia raised an eyebrow, feigning surprise.

Then, Mr. Hassan picked another chit, his eyes widening a bit, a grin forming. "Ah, here's an interesting one. To the delegates of India and Mexico... 'You two look cute together. The committee ships it!'"

The room erupted in a mix of laughter and excited murmurs. Elena and Aarav exchanged an amused glance, their faces turning a shade of crimson. There was an unspoken agreement between them, a silent acknowledgment that, beyond the policy debates and resolution drafting, the conference had forged a connection that neither had anticipated.

As the laughter and teasing continued, Mr. Hassan couldn't resist adding, "Well, there's certainly a United Nations of emotions in this room!" This prompted another round of hearty chuckles.

Ms. Patel, still giggling, waved another chit in the air, teasing the curiosity of the audience. "Alright, next up. To the delegate of Japan, 'Your dedication to detail in your drafts is as mesmerizing as your smile. #DetailingDreams.'"

The delegate from Japan laughed, his cheeks turning a noticeable shade of pink, as he gave a thumbs-up to the room, not sure where to direct it but appreciating the compliment nonetheless.

Mr. Hassan continued, "To the delegate from Brazil, 'Your speech on sustainable agriculture was inspiring.

Let's cultivate a deeper connection? #GrowTogether.'" The delegate from Brazil laughed heartily, acknowledging the witty confession with a mock salute.

Ms. Patel winked at the room before reading the next chit. "To the delegate of Canada, 'Your voice melts away the ice. Warm regards from a secret admirer.' #CanadianWarmth."

The delegate from Canada looked both amused and puzzled, trying to discern who might have sent the mysterious note.

As the readings continued, the atmosphere grew lighter and more relaxed. The delegates, usually so engrossed in serious discussions, now found themselves laughing and joking, a pleasant departure from the rigors of the conference.

Finally, as the last of the confession chits was read out, Ms. Patel clapped her hands together. "Delegates, thank you for indulging in this fun segment. Remember, these connections, be they friendships or more, are what make these conferences special. Let's cherish them."

The room erupted in applause, appreciating the levity of the session. It was a reminder that amidst all the serious work, there was room for fun, laughter, and unexpected connections. The committee had not just connected over policies and politics, but over shared jokes, smiles, and a camaraderie that went beyond their roles as delegates.

The Motion of Entertainment continued, with more confessions, fun activities, and an overall relaxed atmosphere. The tension of the past sessions faded, replaced by a sense of camaraderie and the shared joy of a job well done.

The day's end found the hotel buzzing with a different kind of energy. The weight of committee sessions was lifted, replaced by the electric anticipation of the closing ceremony. The hallways, usually filled with focused delegates discussing policy points, now echoed with laughter and spirited chatter.

Aarav and Elena found themselves in the midst of a group of delegates from various committees, everyone sharing their experiences and recounting the most memorable moments. As they listened to the tales, Aarav's hand brushed against Elena's. A spark of memory passed between them, taking them back to the elevator and the unexpected kiss they had shared.

Elena felt a warm sensation creeping up her cheeks. She risked a glance towards Aarav, who seemed equally affected, a light shade of pink tinting his tan skin. Their eyes met for a fleeting moment, full of shared secrets and unspoken promises. It was clear that, despite the distractions of the MUN, they had been on each other's minds.

However, before either could act or say anything, Ritesh jumped in, recounting a hilarious incident involving a delegate who'd misunderstood a point of procedure. The group erupted in laughter, and the moment between Aarav and Elena was momentarily overshadowed.

As the evening went on, they both mingled, caught up with friends from other committees, and exchanged contacts with new acquaintances. But through it all, Aarav and Elena remained acutely aware of each other's presence, often finding themselves gravitating towards each other, sharing inside jokes and recalling their shared experiences over the past few days.

Later, as the crowd began to thin out, Aarav and Elena found themselves standing near the balcony overlooking the Mumbai skyline. The city's lights shimmered like a sea of stars, and the distant hum of traffic served as a gentle backdrop to their conversation.

Elena leaned against the railing, "You know, these past few days have been something. Between the debates, the resolution, and, well..." she trailed off, a coy smile playing on her lips.

Aarav chuckled, "And the unexpected moments in elevators?"

Elena blushed but held his gaze, "Yes, those too."

Aarav turned to face her fully, leaning slightly against the balcony's edge. The ambient lights cast a soft glow on his face, making his eyes shimmer. "You know, Elena," he began, searching for the right words, "this MUN has been unlike any other for me. It wasn't just about the debates, the resolutions, or even the competition. It was about... us."

Elena looked down, her heart racing. She had felt the same way. The intensity, the connection, and the undeniable chemistry between them had been palpable from the start. "Aarav, I've attended quite a few MUNs, and while they've all been special in their own way, this one... with you, it felt different. It felt... real."

Aarav moved closer, reducing the space between them. "Elena, I've never met anyone quite like you. You're fierce, intelligent, and incredibly passionate. From the moment we started working together, I knew there was something between us, something beyond just committee camaraderie."

Their eyes locked, and for a moment, the world around them seemed to fade away. The distant sounds of the city, the laughter from inside the hotel, everything receded into the background, leaving just the two of them.

The air between them thickened with tension and a magnetic pull drew them closer. Without uttering a word, they leaned into each other, their lips meeting in a fervent embrace. The kiss was tender at first, an exploration, but soon deepened as pent-up emotions surged forth. It was a kiss that spoke of months of silent yearning, of stolen glances, of words unsaid.

Elena's fingers found their way into Aarav's hair, pulling him closer, while Aarav's hands settled on the small of her back, anchoring her to him. Time seemed to stand still as the rest of the world melted away, leaving just the two of them in a cocoon of their own making.

After what felt like an eternity, they broke apart, breathless. Their foreheads resting against each other's, their breaths mingling.

"That was..." Aarav started, his voice a husky whisper.

"Unexpected," Elena finished for him, her eyes still closed, savoring the moment.

A soft chuckle escaped Aarav's lips. "Well, not entirely unexpected."

Elena opened her eyes, meeting his gaze. "True," she admitted with a smile.

They stood like that for a few moments, absorbing the weight of their shared moment, knowing that from this point on, things between them would never be the same.

Around them, the evening was drawing to a close. The night sky was a brilliant tapestry of stars, and the distant sounds of Mumbai continued to play a low hum in the background.

Aarav broke the silence first, his voice thoughtful. "You know, in all the unpredictability of this MUN, I never imagined this."

Elena chuckled softly, "Neither did I. Life has its own plans, doesn't it?"

He nodded, looking out towards the city lights. "Every moment has led up to this, hasn't it? From the start of the conference, the tension, the resolution debates, and then... us."

Elena turned towards him, her gaze earnest. "I believe in serendipity, Aarav. Maybe we were meant to be here, at this very moment. Maybe everything that happened was leading us to this."

He met her gaze, and for a second, words weren't necessary. They both understood what the other was feeling.

"Come on," Elena said after a while, "We should probably head back. Tomorrow is the closing ceremony, after all."

Aarav nodded, offering his arm. "Shall we?"

Elena linked her arm through his, and together, they walked back towards the hotel, the night's revelations weighing on their minds but also filling their hearts with hope for what the future might hold.

Elena entered her room, her cheeks flushed and her heart still racing. The minute she walked in, Isabella, her roommate, burst into a series of giggles.

"I saw that," she teased, wiggling her eyebrows suggestively.

Elena groaned, collapsing onto her bed, her face buried into the pillow. "Oh my god, you saw?"

Isabella sat next to her, giving a playful poke. "Hard to miss. But hey, I'm happy for you. You both seem... right for each other."

Elena sat up, her eyes shining. "It feels like a dream, Isa. It's crazy how life surprises you."

Meanwhile, in his room, Aarav paced back and forth, a myriad of thoughts consuming him. Ritesh looked up from his laptop, observing Aarav's restless demeanor.

"You okay, man?" Ritesh asked, raising an eyebrow.

Aarav ran a hand through his hair. "What if, Ritesh? What if I win tomorrow and it complicates things with Elena? But if I lose, I might risk my future aspirations, yet possibly have something beautiful with her."

Ritesh sighed, setting aside his laptop. "Life's not that binary, Aarav. You're overthinking. You can't control the outcome of the conference, but you can control how you react to it."

Aarav looked up, meeting Ritesh's steady gaze. "It's like choosing between development and sustainability. Both are crucial, but striking a balance seems impossible."

Ritesh nodded, understanding the metaphor. "But remember how in the committee, you and Elena found a middle ground? Sometimes, life works in a similar way. You don't have to choose one over the other. Maybe there's a way to have both."

Aarav pondered over Ritesh's words, taking a deep breath. "Maybe you're right. I should just take things as they come."

Ritesh clapped Aarav on the back. "That's the spirit. Now, get some rest. Tomorrow's a big day."

And as the night deepened, both Elena and Aarav, in their respective rooms, contemplated the uncertainties of the future, hoping that fate would be kind to them.

Harmonies and Horizons

The grand ballroom was adorned with shimmering chandeliers and elegant drapes. Delegates from various committees were seated, murmuring in excitement, awaiting the announcement of the winners. As the final day of the MUN conference, it was the culmination of hard work, passionate debates, and sleepless nights of research.

Amidst the sea of delegates, Aarav and Elena found themselves seated next to each other. Yet, despite their physical closeness, an intangible tension seemed to stretch between them. Elena's fingers nervously drummed on her lap, while Aarav's eyes seemed distant, lost in thought.

Recognizing the underlying anxiety, Aarav slowly reached out, intertwining his fingers with Elena's. She turned to look at him, her blue eyes searching his for reassurance.

He squeezed her hand gently. "It's okay," he whispered, his voice barely audible over the surrounding chatter. "Whatever happens, it will be fine."

Elena gave him a tentative smile, taking comfort in his words, but the unease still lingered.

The lights dimmed, and the Executive Board of each committee took the stage, ready to announce the winners. The room was a mix of hope, anticipation, and nervousness. Each name called was met with applause, some with cheers of joy and others with sighs of disappointment. Ritesh winning in WHO, elated to be the selected for a scholarship programme at Columbia University for social science and public health programme.

As the United Nations Framework Convention on Climate Change (UNFCCC) committee's turn approached, Elena's grip on Aarav's hand tightened. The chairperson began to speak, outlining the accomplishments and challenges faced during the session.

"The dedication and passion shown by each delegate have truly impressed us," the chairperson remarked. "But as always, there are those who've stood out."

The room hung on every word, waiting for the announcement. The names of the honorable mentions were called out, followed by the best delegate from the opposing bloc.

Finally, the moment of truth arrived. "And the Best Delegate for the UNFCCC goes to..."

Elena and Aarav held their breath.

"...Delegate of India, Aarav!"

A roar of applause filled the room. Aarav, momentarily stunned, looked at Elena, his face reflecting a mix of joy and surprise. Elena, tears in her eyes, hugged him tightly. "I knew it," she whispered.

As Aarav made his way to the stage to collect his award, he couldn't help but think about the whirlwind of events over the past few days. The challenges, the unexpected twists, the connection with Elena—everything seemed to fall into place.

Back at their seats, as the ceremony continued, Aarav turned to Elena, his face serious. "This win doesn't change anything between us, Elena. I hope you know that."

Elena nodded, her voice firm. "I do. But right now, let's just celebrate your well-deserved win."

The ceremony came to an end, but for Aarav and Elena, it marked the beginning of a new chapter.

As the final applause died down and the delegates began to mingle, a distinguished-looking gentleman approached Elena, his silver hair contrasting sharply with his dark blue suit. His name tag identified him as Professor Harold Whitman from Stanford University.

"Miss Elena?" he inquired with a raised eyebrow, confirming her identity.

"Yes, that's me," Elena replied, intrigued.

"Ah, excellent! I was quite taken with your performance during the debates. Your insights, your dedication, and your ability to engage with the opposing blocs were truly commendable," he complimented.

Elena blushed slightly, taken aback by the praise. "Thank you, sir. It was quite a learning experience."

Professor Whitman nodded in agreement. "Well, speaking of learning experiences," he began, pausing for dramatic effect, "how would you like to continue your studies at Stanford?"

Elena's eyes widened in surprise. "Are you... are you offering me a scholarship?"

"Yes," Professor Whitman confirmed, "a full scholarship, in fact, to the same program as Aarav. There's just one condition: you'll be assisting me and my team as a research assistant. Your perspective and skills would be invaluable to our ongoing projects."

Elena was momentarily speechless, the weight of the offer sinking in. "Wow, that's... that's an incredible opportunity. Thank you, Professor."

Aarav, overhearing the conversation, walked over, a look of surprise and happiness on his face. "Elena, that's fantastic!" he exclaimed.

The three of them chatted for a while longer, discussing the specifics of the program and the role Elena would play.

As Professor Whitman left the duo, Aarav turned to Elena, his eyes twinkling. "Seems like we might be spending a lot more time together," he teased.

Elena laughed, "Looks like it. I guess the adventure has just begun.

The two of them, standing in the middle of the grand ballroom, with a future of possibilities ahead, shared a hopeful, joyous look, knowing that their paths were now more intertwined than ever.

The ambiance after the closing ceremony was electric with excitement, relief, and the anticipation of farewells. Delegates took pictures, exchanged contact details, and made promises to stay in touch. Amidst this cheerful chaos, Aarav and Elena exchanged a look, silently communicating a desire to escape the crowd for a more private moment.

Walking side by side, they made their way through the hotel corridors, eventually arriving at Aarav's room. He opened the door, revealing a tidy space with a sprawling view of the city's skyline bathed in the soft glow of the setting sun.

Aarav turned on some ambient music, the soft notes of a piano melody filling the room. "Thought we could use some quiet time," he said, taking a seat on the couch and patting the space next to him.

Elena hesitated for a split second before joining him. She was acutely aware of their proximity, her heart thudding loudly against her ribcage.

They sat in silence for a few moments, both lost in their thoughts. The weight of the past few days, the intensity of their experiences both in and out of the committee sessions, and the sudden turn their personal lives had taken made for a lot to process.

Finally, Elena broke the silence, "It's overwhelming, isn't it? The conference, the recognition, the scholarship offer, and... us."

Aarav nodded, turning to face her. "It is. Everything changed so fast. But you know, amidst all the chaos and surprises, I'm glad I met you."

She smiled, her eyes shining. "Me too. But," she hesitated, "what happens now? You're going to Stanford, and so am I, but things are complicated, Aarav. We're entering a new phase of our lives, and while I'm thrilled about the possibilities, I'm also scared."

Aarav took a deep breath, his gaze intense. "Elena, I can't predict the future, and I won't give you empty promises. But I do know one thing: I want to give 'us' a chance. We have something special, and while it's true that the next chapter of our lives will be challenging, I believe we can navigate it together."

Elena looked into his eyes, searching for answers, for certainty. But all she found was sincerity and warmth. Taking a leap of faith, she whispered, "Let's give 'us' a chance then."

The two shared a tender moment, their faces inches apart, and in that quiet room with the golden light streaming in, they sealed their promise with a kiss.

Chasing Dreams, Facing Shadows

The dawn broke with an orange-pink hue, casting soft shadows across the city. The hustle and bustle of the morning was evident as delegates readied themselves to leave, some heading back to their countries, others extending their stay to explore Mumbai a bit more.

Elena was packing her bags, going through the souvenirs she had bought and the mementos she had collected during the MUN. Each item brought back a memory, some of laughter, some of heated debates, and some of the unexpected connection she had made with Aarav.

A soft knock at her door broke her reverie. She opened it to find Aarav, looking dapper as always, though there was a hint of sadness in his eyes.

"I thought I'd come by and drop you off at the airport," he said, trying to keep his voice steady.

Elena smiled gratefully, "That'd be nice."

The journey to the airport was filled with casual chitchat, both trying to steer clear of the impending goodbye. They discussed their plans for the next few months, how they'd prepare for Stanford, and some lighter moments from the conference.

Upon reaching the airport, the atmosphere became more somber. Elena checked in her luggage, and as they waited for her boarding announcement, the weight of their parting settled in.

Facing Aarav, Elena said, "It's strange how in such a short time, people can become so important to you."

Aarav nodded, taking her hands in his, "It's been a whirlwind, but I wouldn't change a thing."

They stood like that for a while, absorbing their last moments together before the long hiatus. As the final boarding call for Elena's flight echoed through the terminal, Aarav pulled her into a tight embrace.

"Promise me we'll stay in touch," he whispered into her ear.

"I promise," Elena replied, her voice choked with emotion. "And in a few months, we'll be in the same place again, navigating the challenges of Stanford together."

They shared one last lingering look, a promise of future meetings, and with a heavy heart, Elena turned to board her flight.

As the plane took off, she looked down at the sprawling city of Mumbai, thinking of the memories she'd made, the lessons she'd learned, and the unexpected love she'd found. With hope in her heart, she looked forward to the next chapter in her life.

Mumbai's dazzling lights seemed almost taunting as Aarav maneuvered his car through the bustling streets, back from the airport. The city, with its cacophonous charm, had always been a backdrop to his life, but tonight, the lights seemed to mockingly highlight fragments of a past he would much rather forget.

His father's memories surged, bringing with them a whirlwind of emotions. There were the days of innocent joy, with Aarav looking up to his father as the pillar of strength, dreaming of emulating his every step. And then there was the aftermath, the devastation that followed his father's betrayal – a wound that still felt fresh.

He pulled over, the weight of the Stanford dream pressing against his chest. Although the scholarship took care of his tuition, Stanford's high living costs stared back at him like a towering peak. How could he promise Elena a shared future when his own was clouded with uncertainty?

Aarav's return home was silent. The lights in his room seemed dimmer, the walls closing in as he was ensnared by the tendrils of his past. There was a knock on the door, soft but persistent. His mother stood there, two cups of steaming chai in hand, her eyes searching his. She had always been his anchor, understanding his unsaid words, his hidden turmoil.

They talked, with Aarav pouring out his anxieties and aspirations. The room grew silent, punctuated only by the soft sips of chai, when she uttered a name he hadn't expected: "Your father."

His initial shock turned to indignation. "After everything he did, Ma?" But her calm demeanor made him reconsider.

His father was, after all, still his father. Perhaps he could help. Yet, the cost of revisiting that painful chapter was high.

The evening was interrupted by the doorbell. The neighbor aunty, always keen on the latest gossip, had come to congratulate them on Aarav's achievement. But even her words felt hollow, overshadowed by the looming decision he had to make.

Later, sitting on the terrace of their apartment, the distant Mumbai lights blinked like a million stars. A soft breeze rustled his hair, bringing with it a surge of determination. He retrieved his phone and, after a moment's hesitation, dialed a number he'd sworn never to call. The rings seemed to last an eternity.

"Hello?"

"Dad," Aarav's voice, firm yet laden with years of suppressed emotions, echoed back. "We need to talk."

Would Aarav's confrontation with his past pave the way for a brighter future? Or would the shadows of bygones hold him back? With Mumbai's vibrant life unfolding below him, Aarav stood at a crossroads, his fate hanging in the balance.

* * * * *

Elena stood by the window of her home, watching as the city lights danced in the distance. A soft wind whispered secrets, and the night held a kind of stillness she hadn't noticed before. Her phone, resting on the table, buzzed again. Hesitantly, she picked it up, her heart racing. The message was from an unknown number, and the threatening words stared back at her:

"If you step foot in Stanford, you'll regret it."

A chill ran down her spine. She had already been rattled by a similar message the previous day. Who was this? What did they want? And why target her?

Elena lived with her abuela, a kind, old woman who had been her pillar of strength after her parents' demise. Their home was filled with memories, laughter, and tales of old. It was a place of safety, warmth, and love. The sudden threat was like a bolt from the blue, casting a dark cloud over her bright future.

The scholarship to Stanford wasn't just about education; it was her ticket to a better life, a way to ensure that her abuela's sacrifices weren't in vain. But now, an unknown adversary was trying to snatch that dream away, shrouding it in fear and uncertainty.

She thought of Aarav, the connection they'd forged, the dreams they'd woven together. She wanted to confide in him, lean on his strength. But she had also seen the weight he carried – the financial burdens, the emotional scars, and the looming specter of his father's legacy. How could she add to his troubles? Especially when he was at such a pivotal juncture in his life.

Time was running out. Her bags were packed, her flight pre-booked. Leaving for Stanford was supposed to be the start of a new chapter, but now it felt like she was stepping into a maze, blindfolded and alone.

As she hugged her abuela goodbye, Elena felt the old woman's strength seep into her. "Life will always have its challenges, mija," her abuela whispered, her voice filled with a wisdom only life could give. "But remember, you carry the strength of all who came before you. You will find your way."

The airport was a blur. Check-ins, security checks, final calls; all done robotically as Elena's mind raced. She sent a quick text to Aarav: *"Take care. Remember our promise. See you in Stanford. ❤"*

She hoped he'd understand the unspoken words, the layers beneath that message. For now, they both had battles to face, roads to navigate. But deep down, she clung to the hope that their paths would converge again, in a place where dreams thrived, and shadows of the past faded away.

* * * * *

Part II

EMBRACING DESTINY

The San Francisco International Airport was bustling with energy, but for Aarav, the noise and chaos faded as he took a moment to breathe it all in. The fragrance of a fresh beginning was unmistakable. Leaving Mumbai and its tangled memories behind, he was here, ready to embrace a new chapter.

Dragging his luggage, Aarav navigated through the exit, still adjusting to the realization that he was now at Stanford. The deal with his father had been a difficult one, fraught with old tensions and new understandings. But it had paved the way for this journey.

As he looked around for a cab, a familiar face caught his attention. Elena! There she was, a radiant vision with her hair cascading down, wearing a light summer dress that seemed to dance with the Californian breeze. Parked beside her was a modest second-hand car, hinting at the life she had begun building here.

Their eyes met, and the distance of months vanished. Elena ran towards him, and they wrapped each other in a warm, lingering embrace, right in the middle of the hustle and bustle. The world seemed to blur and slow down; all that mattered was this connection, this moment.

"Surprise!" Elena's voice was soft, her eyes twinkling.

Aarav laughed, his eyes moist, "You never cease to amaze me."

"Thought I'd save you from the cab fare," she winked, referring to her car. "Been saving up from the job I started a few months ago."

They loaded Aarav's bags into the car and set off, the journey alive with their chatter and laughter. It was evident that while they had been continents apart, their bond had only deepened. Their texts and calls had bridged the distance, keeping the ember of their connection alive.

"You look different," Aarav mused, glancing at her as they drove.

"Different good or different bad?" Elena teased.

"Different beautiful," he replied with a grin, making her blush.

The drive from the airport to Stanford was a visual delight. The Californian landscape unfurled like a canvas painted in broad strokes of green and gold. The highway was fringed with tall eucalyptus trees, their leaves rustling with every gust, creating a serene, musical backdrop.

Elena took the scenic route, wanting Aarav to absorb the beauty of the Bay Area. Rolling hills covered in a blanket of wildflowers stretched on one side while on the other, glimpses of the shimmering blue waters of the Pacific Ocean sparkled under the sun.

As they approached the Silicon Valley region, orchards filled with apple and cherry trees became more frequent, their blossoms lending a sweet fragrance to the air. The roads meandered, flanked by vineyards with rows upon rows of grapevines, promising bottles of exquisite Californian wine.

Aarav, accustomed to the metropolitan congestion of Mumbai, was taken aback by the vast open spaces, the sprawling landscapes, and the orderly urban structures. "It's breathtaking," he murmured, his eyes wide with wonder.

Elena smiled, taking pleasure in his amazement. "I thought you'd like it. The landscape here has a way of making you dream bigger."

The drive was therapeutic. The rhythmic hum of the car's engine combined with the natural beauty was mesmerizing. As they cruised along, a serene silence settled between them, allowing them to simply soak in the surroundings and the moment.

Soon, the iconic Hoover Tower of Stanford University began to pierce the sky in the distance. The sight of it made Aarav's heart race with excitement and a hint of nervousness. It was a symbol of the new journey he was embarking on, and having Elena by his side made it all the more special.

As the car pulled into the campus, Aarav was lost in thought, taking in the beauty of the place that would be his home for the next few years. The terracotta roofs, palm-lined pathways, and majestic sandstone buildings – it was a world away from the streets of Mumbai, yet it felt strangely familiar, like he was returning to a place he had always belonged.

They drove through Stanford's Main Quad, a picturesque expanse of lush lawns and architectural marvels. The Quad, with its Romanesque arches and meticulously manicured gardens, seemed to Aarav like the heart of an ancient academic realm.

Elena, seeing his fascination, remarked, "Wait till you see it during sunset. The whole place takes on this golden hue. It's magical."

Aarav chuckled, "Given how gorgeous it looks now, I can hardly imagine it becoming more beautiful."

Parking her car near Wilbur Hall, Elena turned to Aarav. "Ready for a quick tour, or do you want to settle in first?"

Still trying to absorb the magnificence around him, Aarav replied, "A quick tour sounds perfect."

Elena took him through the key spots on campus – the iconic Memorial Church with its intricate mosaics, the sprawling Green Library, and the serene Lake Lagunita, where students often picnicked or studied on sunny days. Every corner of Stanford seemed to have its own story, and Elena narrated snippets of her past three months, filling him in on her experiences and the little quirks of life at Stanford.

It was during this walk that Aarav realized the change in Elena. While she retained her warmth and radiant smile, there was a newfound confidence in her stride, a shimmer of self-assuredness in her eyes. Stanford had already started molding her.

They concluded their tour at the Coupa Café, a favorite hangout spot for students. Over steaming cups of coffee, they delved deeper into their experiences over the past few months. Elena talked about her job, the challenges, the small victories, and the satisfaction of being self-reliant.

Aarav listened intently, occasionally interjecting with his own tales of last-minute preparations, the emotional farewells back home, and his whirlwind reconciliation with his father.

As afternoon turned to evening, the sun cast elongated shadows across the campus, painting everything in a rich golden light. Sitting there, time seemed to slow as the weight of their shared journey settled on them. They were no longer just individuals with personal dreams. Their stories had intertwined, making them partners in this new chapter of life.

Elena finally broke the silence, "I've got a surprise for you."

Aarav raised an eyebrow, intrigued, "Oh?"

With a mischievous smile, she replied, "But that will have to wait till tomorrow."

As they headed back to Elena's car, the day's exhaustion began to catch up with Aarav. But amidst the fatigue, his heart was light, filled with gratitude for the journey so far and anticipation for what lay ahead.

As the evening's warm glow illuminated Stanford, Elena's phone emitted a sudden ding, cutting through their shared moment of serenity. Her face paled slightly as she glanced at the screen. Without a word, she quickly turned the phone face-down and slid it into her bag.

Aarav noticed the abrupt change in her demeanor. "Everything okay?" he asked, concern evident in his voice.

Elena forced a smile, though her eyes betrayed a hint of anxiety. "Yeah, just a message from work. I'll deal with it later."

He nodded, though not entirely convinced. They had always shared an open communication, but he sensed she was holding something back. He made a mental note to ask her about it later, respecting her need for privacy at that moment.

As they continued walking, Aarav's mind raced with questions. What had caused such a reaction in Elena? Was she in some sort of trouble? Or was it something personal she wasn't ready to share?

However, trusting Elena's judgment, he chose not to push further. But deep down, a seed of worry had been planted, foreshadowing complexities in the days to come.

That night, as Aarav settled into his dorm, the sounds of Stanford humming in the background, he realized he wasn't alone in this new world. With Elena by his side, it felt like home. The challenges of the past seemed smaller, and the future, though uncertain, looked promising. The adventure had only just begun.

Once they had lugged Aarav's belongings into his new dorm, the energy between them shifted. The room was a small, cozy space with a single bed, a study desk, and a window that looked out onto a sprawling green quad. The setting sun painted the room in warm hues, enhancing the ambiance.

Aarav turned to face Elena, his eyes tracing the familiar curves of her face. He took a deep breath, drinking in her presence after what felt like an eternity. Slowly, he reached out, cradling her face in his hands.

Elena met his gaze, her hazel eyes reflecting the depth of her emotions. The world seemed to fade as the space between them diminished. Aarav leaned in, gently pressing his lips to hers. Elena responded instantly, deepening the kiss as her hands slid up to tangle in his hair.

The kiss was intense and full of longing, a culmination of months of separation and the myriad emotions that had swirled between them. They lost themselves in the moment, each pouring their hearts out, letting the physical connection express what words often failed to convey.

After what felt like hours, they broke apart, slightly breathless. Their foreheads rested against each other, eyes still closed, savoring the lingering warmth of their embrace.

Elena whispered, her voice shaky, "I missed you, Aarav."

He smiled, brushing a stray hair behind her ear, "I missed you too, more than you could imagine."

They stood there for a few more minutes, wrapped in each other's arms, letting the weight of the moment sink in. For now, the complexities of the past and the uncertainties of the future faded, replaced by the bliss of being reunited. But unknown to Aarav, shadows from Elena's recent past threatened to cloud their newfound happiness.

Elena sighed deeply, leaning into Aarav's embrace. There was a comforting warmth about him, a stability she had yearned for during the turbulent months leading up to this reunion.

"How's life been in Stanford, without me?" Aarav teased, trying to lighten the mood.

Elena chuckled, "Exciting but lonely. This place is vast, filled with incredible minds and endless opportunities. But without you, it felt incomplete."

Aarav smiled, his heart swelling with warmth. "Well, I'm here now. We'll make memories together."

As the evening darkened, Elena suggested they take a stroll around the campus. Stanford University, with its Spanish architecture and sprawling gardens, was a sight to behold, especially under the moonlit sky. They walked hand in hand, laughing and sharing stories of their time apart.

However, as they wandered through the Main Quad, Elena's phone vibrated, interrupting the tranquil ambiance. She quickly pulled it from her pocket and glanced at the screen. Her face paled, and a shadow of worry crossed her features. Hurriedly, she put it away, hoping Aarav hadn't noticed.

But he had. "Is everything okay?" he inquired, sensing her sudden change in demeanor.

Elena hesitated for a moment before offering a reassuring smile. "Yeah, just some work stuff. Nothing to worry about."

But Aarav wasn't convinced. He remembered the moment in the car when her phone had dinged, and she'd hastily set it aside. Sensing her reluctance to share, he decided not to push. Perhaps she needed time, he thought.

The evening came to an end with a quiet dinner at a nearby café. Both seemed lost in their thoughts, each guarding secrets they weren't ready to share.

As they parted ways, with promises to meet the next day, the weight of their individual burdens was palpable. What lay ahead was uncertain, but their bond was undeniable. The challenges they would face in the coming days would test the strength of their relationship and define their shared future.

* * * * *

THE PRICE OF DREAMS

The humid air of Mumbai hung heavy as Aarav stepped into the dimly lit room. The strong aroma of cigar smoke filled the space, blending with the mellow scent of aged whiskey. At the far end, a familiar silhouette leaned against a window, overlooking the bustling streets below.

"Sit," the voice was firm, almost a command, not betraying any emotion.

Aarav took a deep breath and settled into a leather chair. The room was adorned with lavish decor, a testament to the wealth and power that resided here. The irony wasn't lost on Aarav – this opulence had once been a part of his world, before it all came crashing down.

His father, Rajan, finally turned to face him, the ambient light revealing a face marked by age and hard choices. His eyes, once bright and full of life, now held a dullness. Yet, an unmistakable fire still burned within.

"It's been a while," Rajan stated, his voice holding a hint of reproach.

Aarav met his gaze, his own eyes mirroring a blend of resentment and desperation. "It has. But I'm here now."

Rajan poured himself a drink, the liquid gold glinting in his glass. "I hear you need help," he said after a long sip, his eyes never leaving Aarav.

Swallowing his pride, Aarav nodded. "Yes. To get to Stanford."

A smirk played on Rajan's lips. "Always the ambitious one. Just like me."

There was an uncomfortable silence. Aarav mustered the courage and finally spoke, "What do you want in return?"

Rajan's face became serious. "When you're done with Stanford, you'll come back and take over the business."

Aarav's heart sank. He was well aware of the nature of his father's dealings. While the facade was that of a successful import-export business, the underbelly was rife with shady deals, corruption, and ties to the underworld. It was the life Aarav had vowed to stay away from.

"That's the price of my help," Rajan continued, his voice cold. "Stanford for the business."

Aarav was trapped. The opportunity to study at Stanford was his dream, but the cost seemed too high. He remembered the nights when his mother cried herself to sleep, the days they went hungry, all because of this business. Could he really plunge himself back into this world?

Rajan leaned in, his eyes piercing into Aarav's soul. "It's a simple choice, son. Your dream or your principles."

Torn between the weight of his ambitions and the pull of his morals, Aarav finally spoke, his voice barely above a whisper, "Alright, I'll do it."

Rajan leaned back, a satisfied smile playing on his lips. "Good. I knew you'd make the right choice."

As Aarav left the room, the weight of his decision bore down on him. He had secured his future at Stanford, but at what cost? The shadows of his father's world would forever loom over him, waiting for his return.

* * * * *

The nights at Stanford had a tranquil quality to them. The campus, bathed in moonlight, seemed to hold within its walls countless dreams and aspirations of generations. Elena, however, found herself far from the embrace of this serenity.

Sitting in her small dorm room, the soft glow of her desk lamp illuminated the sharp lines of concern etched onto her face. Her phone lay beside her, its screen casting an eerie blue hue. She hesitated, her fingers trembling slightly, then unlocked the device to view the most recent message:

Elena, we warned you about coming to Stanford. Now that your dear Aarav is here, it might just be two birds with one stone. If you value his life, you know what to do. Leave.

The words seemed to jump out at her, each one like a dagger piercing her heart. The feeling of being watched, of being hunted, was oppressive, choking the joy out of her reunion with Aarav.

She scrolled up, reviewing the previous threats. They had started off as vague warnings but had progressively become more direct and menacing. Whoever was behind this seemed to have a vast reach, to know the intimate details of her life, even here at Stanford.

A flood of emotions overwhelmed Elena: anger, fear, frustration. Why her? What had she done to deserve this? And how did they know about Aarav? She remembered the whispered conversations back home, rumors about a rival business faction that had been at odds with her family for generations. Could they be behind this? Was this their way of getting back at her family by targeting her?

She thought of confiding in Aarav, of sharing the weight of this secret. But the very mention of his name in the threat paralyzed her. She couldn't bear the thought of putting him in more danger than he already was.

Closing her eyes, she took a deep breath, attempting to calm the storm within. She had to be strategic. Responding to the threat or even acknowledging it could escalate the situation. She needed help, but who could she trust? The campus police? An old family friend? Or perhaps a private investigator?

She decided to keep a low profile for the time being, hoping that this was just an empty threat. But deep down, she knew she was in a high-stakes game, and the safety of Aarav and herself hung in the balance.

As the night wore on, Elena finally drifted into a restless sleep, her dreams haunted by shadowy figures and the chilling words of the message. The promise of a fresh start at Stanford now seemed tainted by the specter of her past, threatening to destroy everything she held dear.

The following day was filled with the thrill of exploration. The Stanford campus buzzed with excitement as new students settled in, each one eager to carve out their unique path in this storied institution.

Elena and Aarav began their day at the Green Library, Stanford's main library. Its imposing facade and intricate architecture promised treasures of knowledge within. Once inside, they were awestruck by the vastness of the collection. Towering shelves laden with books from every conceivable discipline stretched as far as the eye could see.

They settled into a cozy nook, surrounded by books on international relations. Aarav pulled out a volume on global political dynamics while Elena immersed herself in a treatise on international peacekeeping operations. Their mutual passion for their chosen field was evident in their animated discussions.

"I've heard Professor Harrison is an authority on peace negotiations," Elena mentioned, looking up from her book. "I'm hoping to take his seminar next semester."

Aarav nodded, "Yeah, and Dr. Sharma is reputed for her work on global economic policies. I've always admired her research. Can't wait to attend her lectures!"

As the day progressed, they met a few seniors from the International Relations program. Their insights and anecdotes about professors, courses, and research opportunities painted a vivid picture of the journey that lay ahead.

The seniors were impressed by Elena and Aarav's enthusiasm and dedication. One of them, a tall, bespectacled guy named Raj, even offered to be their mentor. "This program can be intense," he warned, "but with the right guidance, you'll sail through. Always here to help!"

The day flew by, and soon, the golden hues of the evening sky enveloped Stanford. The duo decided to wind down and head to Elena's dorm.

Upon arriving, Elena pulled out a tub of mint chocolate chip ice cream from her mini-fridge. They laughed, shared stories, and indulged in the creamy delight, momentarily forgetting the weight of the world around them. The camaraderie between them was palpable, a shared bond that seemed to grow stronger with each passing moment.

Elena's face lit up with a mischievous glint as she playfully dabbed a bit of ice cream on Aarav's nose, leading to a mini ice cream war in the room. Their laughter echoed, a testament to the happiness of the moment.

But as the evening deepened, the stark contrast between the joy of the present and the shadows of their individual pasts became even more pronounced. Both were, in their own way, battling inner demons, and the coming days would test the strength of their bond and resilience.

The last of the evening sunbeams filtered through Elena's window, casting a warm, amber glow across the room. A soft, melodic tune emanated from a nearby speaker, the haunting notes of a love song filling the space. As the lyrics wove tales of longing, hope, and passion, the atmosphere grew more intimate, more ethereal.

Elena, her fingers still sticky from the ice cream, whispered a quote she'd read once, her voice a gentle caress,

"Love isn't just a feeling, it's an art. And like any art, it takes not only inspiration but also a lot of work."

Aarav, clearly moved, responded with a line of his own, "Love is the poetry of the senses. When it's true and deep, it becomes the very essence of our existence." The sincerity in his eyes mirrored the depth of his words.

Time seemed to slow. They moved closer, their eyes locked, searching each other's souls. The connection between them was palpable, a magnetic pull that neither could resist. In that instant, the world outside ceased to exist.

Elena began to recite a poem she'd written a while back:

"*In the dance of twilight, amidst shadow and sun,*
Two souls converge, seemingly becoming one.
Drawn by fate, destined to intertwine,
In the vast tapestry of time."

Aarav was captivated by her words. He softly replied with his own verse:

"*In the silent symphony of the night,*
I found solace in your luminous light.
Together, we challenge the infinite expanse,
With love as our eternal dance."

With the song's chorus rising in crescendo, Elena reached out, taking Aarav's hand, leading him to the center of her room. They began to dance, moving in rhythm with the music, lost in each other.

The world outside, with all its chaos and uncertainty, faded away. In that room, in that moment, only love mattered. Only they existed. And as the song reached its poignant end, their lips met in a kiss that spoke of promises, dreams, and endless tomorrows.

It was a moment suspended in time, a memory etched in eternity. A testament to the magic that happens when two souls find their way to one another.

In the dim, golden-lit room, every sensation seemed heightened. The soft hum of the air conditioner in the background, the distant chirping of crickets, and the rustle of leaves outside the window merged into a symphony that underscored their shared emotion.

Elena's fingers traced the lines of Aarav's face, feeling the warmth of his skin, the steady pulse beneath. Their breaths mingled, eyes searching for unspoken words in each other's depths. Each touch, each glance was a whispered secret, an intimate promise of understanding and connection.

"I never realized," Aarav murmured, his voice rough with emotion, "that life could hold moments like this. Moments where everything else fades away, and there's just... us."

Elena smiled, her eyes misty. "We're made of stardust, you and I," she whispered back. "Billions of years of cosmic history have led to this singular moment. And in the vastness of the universe, it's our love that has made this moment infinite."

His fingers tangled in her hair, pulling her closer until their foreheads touched. They breathed in tandem, the very air between them charged with electricity. Each beat of their hearts, now synced in rhythm, echoed a profound connection that transcended words.

The emotional intensity was overwhelming, consuming. Both had faced their individual battles and insecurities, yet in this instant, they felt invincible, bound together by a force that defied logic and reason.

Elena's voice was soft but filled with conviction, "No matter the challenges we face, no matter the storms that try to break us, our love will remain. It's the anchor that grounds us, the light that guides us."

Aarav pulled her into a tender embrace, burying his face in the crook of her neck. "In you, I've found my harbor, my solace. Every scar, every wound I've ever had, feels healed when I'm with you."

Their lips met again, the kiss deepening, fueled by a passion that had been building since their paths first crossed. It was a kiss of promises and dreams, of past heartaches and future hopes. In that intimate union, two souls, each with their own intricate tapestry of experiences, became irrevocably intertwined.

As the night deepened and the world outside continued its relentless pace, inside that room, time stood still. Two hearts, having found their match, reveled in the magic of love's all-encompassing embrace.

The warmth of their shared embrace gradually lulled Aarav into a fitful sleep. As the boundaries between reality and dreams blurred, he was thrust back into the dark alleys of his childhood memories.

* * * * *

FROM DUSK TILL DAWN

The room was dimly lit, the only source of illumination being the cold, sterile light from the streetlamp outside. The wallpaper, once bright and cheerful, now bore the marks of time and neglect. Shadows danced across the floor, playing out the horrors of the past.

He was hiding behind the old wooden cabinet, his young fingers clamped over his mouth to stifle the sobs that threatened to escape. The sounds of anger and aggression echoed, filling the room with an oppressive weight. His mother's muffled cries, the harsh tone of his father's voice, and the sickening thud of a blow landing all mixed in a cacophony of pain and fear.

Suddenly, he felt a firm grip on his arm. Young Aarav was yanked from his hiding spot, his father's furious eyes boring into his. The bitterness, anger, and disappointment in those eyes struck him harder than any physical blow ever could.

The nightmarish scene shifted. Aarav, now older, stood at the doorway, watching as his mother painstakingly covered her bruises with makeup, tears streaming silently down her face. The weight of unspoken pain and the depth of her sacrifice bore down on him, an unbearable burden of guilt and helplessness.

He jolted awake, his breathing ragged, sweat beading on his forehead. The ghostly remnants of the dream clung to him, the emotions raw and palpable.

Elena, feeling the sudden movement, woke up to find Aarav in the throes of his night terror. Concern filled her eyes as she gently cupped his face, her voice a soothing balm, "Aarav, it's okay. You're safe now. I'm here."

He clung to her, his strong frame shaking with the aftershocks of the dream. With every comforting stroke of her hand on his back, every whispered assurance, the demons of the past retreated.

"Elena," he began, voice choked with emotion, "there are things... things about my past that you don't know."

She gently brushed his hair from his forehead, her gaze unwavering. "When you're ready to share, I'm here to listen. But for now, just know that I'm here for you. Always."

Holding onto each other, they sought solace in their shared warmth, the quiet reassurance of their bond pushing away the shadows of the past. And as the first light of dawn began to seep through the curtains, hope and love reigned supreme, promising a brighter tomorrow.

The morning light cascaded through the dorm room's window, casting a golden glow on the entwined forms of

Aarav and Elena. The events of the previous night, marked with deep emotions and revelations, seemed like a distant memory in the serene embrace of the new day.

They stirred, the world outside beckoning them to start anew. Aarav stretched, the vestiges of sleep still evident in his eyes, and watched as Elena, with a playful glint in her eyes, slipped on one of his oversized hoodies. The navy fabric draped over her, a comfortable embrace that made her look both adorable and mischievous.

"You planning on returning that?" Aarav teased, pointing at the hoodie.

Elena twirled around, giving him a mock model pose. "What do you think? I believe I wear it better."

He laughed, the sound rich and genuine, "Indeed you do."

After sharing a quick, refreshing shower, they headed out, the Stanford campus alive with activity. Students rushing to classes, the distant hum of conversations, and the general vibrancy created a backdrop for their morning.

Upon Elena's recommendation, they chose a quaint little café nestled between two large academic buildings. It was a popular spot known for its artisanal coffees and fresh pastries. As they stepped inside, the aroma of freshly brewed coffee enveloped them, promising a comforting start to the day.

They found a cozy corner spot, the wooden table worn down by countless coffees and conversations of students past. Aarav opted for a cappuccino, while Elena chose her favorite lavender latte. As they waited for their order, they shared a croissant, the flaky layers perfectly complementing the rich buttery interior.

"So," Elena began, taking a sip of her latte, "What's the plan for today?"

Aarav leaned back, thoughtful. "I was hoping to visit the International Relations department, maybe meet some of the professors. And later, perhaps explore the campus a bit?"

Elena nodded in agreement, "Sounds perfect. And maybe in the evening, we can catch a movie or something. Make the most of our time before the academic grind starts."

Aarav reached across the table, entwining his fingers with hers. "Sounds like a plan. But honestly, as long as I'm with you, any plan sounds perfect."

She blushed, the rosy hue matching the playful glint in her eyes. "Always the charmer, aren't you?"

Their laughter rang out, easy and genuine. As they made plans for the day, the world outside seemed brighter, promising endless possibilities. And while challenges lay ahead, for now, they reveled in the joy of each other's company, cherishing the moments that made life worth living.

The afternoon sun streamed into the International Relations department's elegant old building. Tall windows framed views of green expanses, while inside, the halls resonated with the muffled discussions of academicians and scholars.

Aarav, now dressed in a sharp navy-blue suit with a crisp white shirt, felt a rush of excitement as he made his way to the office of the head of the department. With each step, he couldn't help but marvel at the rich history of the place, the walls adorned with plaques and portraits of distinguished alumni.

Professor Reynolds, a distinguished-looking man in his sixties with salt-and-pepper hair, welcomed Aarav into his book-lined office. Their conversation was insightful, touching upon the nuances of the program and the expectations. Aarav felt a kinship with Professor Reynolds, sensing that he was not just an academician but also a mentor who genuinely cared about his students.

Meanwhile, Elena had sequestered herself in one of the library's quiet study rooms. Surrounded by stacks of books and her laptop, she meticulously pored over the latest research articles and data related to her subject. The hours flew by, but she was invigorated by the depth and breadth of knowledge available at her fingertips.

As the evening approached, Aarav sent a text: *"All done here. Ready for our movie date?"*

Elena responded with a smiley, *"Absolutely! Meet you at the Rodin Sculpture Garden in 15?"*

Meeting at the garden, a peaceful spot known for its captivating sculptures and tranquil ambiance, felt perfect. As Aarav waited, he took a moment to appreciate the serene beauty around him, the gentle hum of conversation from other students serving as a soft backdrop.

Elena approached, her face lit up by the soft evening glow. "All set for our cinematic adventure?" she teased.

Aarav chuckled, "Always. I even got us tickets to that new indie film you mentioned."

They headed to the campus movie theater, a vintage building that exuded old-world charm. As they settled into the plush seats, the lights dimmed, transporting them into a world of drama, emotion, and storytelling.

The film was a heartfelt drama about love, loss, and finding oneself. As the credits rolled, both Aarav and Elena were silent, lost in their thoughts, the movie's message resonating deeply with them.

As they stepped out into the cool night, Aarav remarked, "That film... it reminded me of us, in a way. Our journey, our struggles, our hopes."

Elena nodded, "It's amazing how art can capture the essence of life so beautifully."

Walking back, hand in hand, under the canopy of stars, they realized that their story, like the movie, was still unfolding. With each passing day, they were adding new chapters, filled with love, challenges, and endless possibilities.

In the soft ambient light of Aarav's room, a gentle classical track flowed from the speakers, the music intertwining with the silence that had settled between them. The room was filled with an air of vulnerability. Elena, her head resting on Aarav's chest, felt the rhythmic beat of his heart, a silent testament to the life he'd led and the secrets he held.

Taking a deep breath, Aarav began, "You know, Elena, every person has a story, some parts of which are harder to share than others." His fingers played with her hair, the gentle caress reassuring himself as much as her.

Elena tightened her grip on him, silently urging him on, "You can tell me anything, Aarav."

The memories surged forward, and Aarav's voice became distant, as if he was reliving the past. "Growing up, my father was everything to me. He was charismatic, powerful, the center of my universe. But then, everything changed."

He paused, swallowing hard, "I remember the nights when I would be jolted awake by the sounds of raised voices. The image that haunts me to this day is seeing my mother, bruised and battered, tears streaming down her face, while my father, drunk and enraged, would storm out."

The weight of the past bore down on him, but Aarav continued, his voice breaking occasionally. "I was torn between idolizing the man who was my father and hating the monster he became during those nights. It confused me, filled me with anger and resentment. I couldn't understand how someone could profess to love their family and yet hurt them in such a way."

Elena felt a tear escape her eye. She lifted her head to look at Aarav. His face was etched with pain, the shadows of his past visible in his eyes. Pulling him close, she whispered, "You're not him, Aarav. You're so much more. You're kind, compassionate, and loving."

Aarav looked into Elena's eyes, "But that's what scares me the most, Elena. The fear that I might become him. That the same blood that runs in his veins runs in mine."

Elena cupped his face, "Aarav, our past shapes us, but it doesn't define us. You have the power to choose your own path, to break the cycle."

As the classical music reached its crescendo, the two of them held onto each other tightly, drawing strength and comfort. It was a moment of raw emotion, of opening up old wounds and finding healing in shared pain.

Before Aarav knew Elena was in deep slumber. The room was dimly lit, only the soft glow of the laptop illuminating Aarav's face. The delicate hum of the air conditioner and the distant sounds of the Stanford night created a peaceful backdrop. Elena lay sprawled across the bed, the steady rise and fall of her chest a testament to her deep slumber. A strand of her hair had fallen over her face, and the serenity that enveloped her was almost ethereal.

Aarav's fingers danced over the keys, piecing together arguments and thoughts for his research paper. Every so often, he'd stop, look up, and let his gaze rest on Elena. The sheer innocence and vulnerability she displayed in her sleep were endearing. A soft smile would play on his lips as he took in the sight – Elena, wrapped up in his hoodie, looking every bit the angel she was to him.

The weight of the earlier conversation still hung in the air. Sharing such a deeply personal and painful part of his past had been challenging, but Elena's unwavering support and understanding made it bearable. He couldn't help but wonder what he had done to deserve someone so understanding and compassionate.

Lost in his thoughts, he typed a sentence, then promptly deleted it, finding it hard to concentrate. The screen displayed a jumble of words, but his mind was elsewhere, reminiscing their journey together and the challenges they'd overcome.

The hours ticked by, and the first rays of dawn began to filter into the room. Elena stirred, mumbling something in her sleep. Aarav saved his document, realizing he wouldn't get much work done tonight. He shut his laptop, stood up, and stretched, feeling the strain in his muscles.

Walking over to the bed, he carefully adjusted the blanket over Elena, ensuring she was warm and comfortable. Then, with a sigh, he slid into bed next to her, wrapping an arm around her waist. Feeling the warmth of her body against his, he closed his eyes, and soon the fatigue of the night took over, pulling him into a deep sleep.

* * * * *

Soft Power, Hard Choices

The Stanford sun was bright and promising as the sprawling campus buzzed with the energy of New Student Orientation. Streams of eager students moved about, taking in the beauty of the historical buildings, the pristine lawns, and the sense of history that hung in the air.

Aarav, dressed in a comfortable pair of jeans and a crisp white shirt, looked every bit the excited freshman. His eyes sparkled with enthusiasm as they darted around, soaking in the sights and sounds of his new academic home.

Elena, on the other hand, had a distinct tightness around her eyes. Her face, usually so full of life, looked drained. Every now and then, her phone would buzz in her pocket, sending a fresh wave of anxiety over her. While Aarav was lost in the wonders of the campus, she was fighting an internal battle, struggling to keep her fears at bay.

Aarav noticed Elena's grip on his hand tighten. "Everything okay?" he asked, genuine concern evident in his voice.

She forced a smile, "Just... overwhelmed, I guess."

It was partly true. Stanford was a dream for both of them. But while Aarav saw a world of possibilities, Elena saw potential threats lurking around every corner. Her phone buzzed again, making her jump. She quickly silenced it, but not before Aarav caught the look of panic on her face.

"Elena, what's going on?" he asked, pulling her aside to a quieter spot.

She hesitated, biting her lip. "It's nothing, really. Just some silly messages."

Aarav frowned, "Show me."

Reluctantly, Elena handed over her phone. As Aarav scrolled through the messages, his face darkened. The threats were explicit, and the mention of his name made his blood run cold. "Why didn't you tell me about this?" he demanded.

"I didn't want to worry you," she admitted, her eyes glistening with tears. "And I thought... I hoped it was just some stupid prank."

Aarav pulled her into a tight embrace, trying to offer some semblance of protection and comfort. "We'll figure this out," he whispered, determination lacing his voice.

They rejoined the throng of students, but the atmosphere had shifted. No longer was it just about the joys of starting a new chapter in their lives. Now, they had to watch their backs, always on guard, always wondering who might be the faceless enemy behind the threats.

As the NSO program began, with professors and seniors addressing the new batch, Aarav and Elena tried to focus on the present, but the shadows of their past and the uncertainty of the future made it a challenge. They clung to each other, drawing strength and solace, reminding themselves that together, they could face any storm.

The mood was somber when Aarav arrived at Elena's dorm. The campus, which had seemed so inviting and vibrant earlier, now felt like a maze of secrets, shadows lurking in the corners. As he knocked on the door, he ran his hand through his hair, trying to calm the storm of thoughts raging within.

Elena opened the door, her face still etched with worry. Without a word, Aarav stepped in and wrapped her in his arms. They stood like that for a moment, drawing comfort from each other's presence.

Elena broke the silence, her voice barely a whisper. "What are we going to do, Aarav?"

Aarav sighed, letting her go and pacing the room. "We need to find out who's behind these messages."

"But how?"

He smirked slightly, a glint of mischief in his eyes. "Well, you might not know this, but I was quite the computer whiz back in the day."

Elena looked at him incredulously. "You? The Mr. MUN and international relations guru?"

He laughed. "Surprising, I know. But before MUNs took over my life, I was deeply into coding and, well, a bit of ethical hacking."

Elena raised an eyebrow, impressed. "So you can trace the number?"

"I can certainly try."

Aarav took out his laptop, setting it on Elena's desk. He began typing furiously, lines of code flying across the screen. Elena watched in awe, seeing a side of Aarav she had never known before. She was reminded, yet again, of the depths and layers that made up this man she had come to care so deeply for.

After what felt like hours, Aarav leaned back, staring at the screen. "Got it."

"Where's it from?" Elena asked, her heart racing.

Aarav's expression was grave. "The number is registered in Pakistan."

Elena's eyes widened. "Pakistani? But Pakistan? Who in Pakistani would want to threaten us?"

Aarav looked pensive and it struck him and he said in a deep voice, "Farhan"

* * * * *

Farhan's POV

Farhan's hands trembled with rage as he scrolled through photos of Aarav, memories of the MUN flooding back. He had been the star delegate for Pakistan and had dreamed of the scholarship to Stanford. But Aarav had overshadowed him, rising to fame within the MUN circuit.

In Farhan's twisted mind, he was convinced that Aarav had been the cause of his suspension. The altercation he had with the delegate from Israel was, in his eyes, just a minor disagreement. But Aarav's rising popularity and the whispering rumors had led Farhan to believe that Aarav had somehow plotted against him, complaining to the organizers and ultimately costing Farhan his reputation.

Every night, Farhan replayed that conference in his mind. The applause for Aarav, the disdainful looks he received, and his dreams crumbling. The scholarship that Aarav received was supposed to be his, and Farhan believed Aarav had stolen his future.

"Revenge," he whispered to himself, staring at Aarav and Elena's smiling faces on the screen. "You took everything from me, Aarav. Now I'll take everything from you."

* * * * *

Elena's face paled as Aarav showed her the results. "Farhan? But...why would he...?"

Aarav sighed deeply, running a hand through his hair. "He thinks I'm the reason he was suspended from the conference. He believes that scholarship should've been his."

Elena looked horrified. "But that altercation wasn't your fault! He was aggressive with the Israeli delegate."

"I know," Aarav said, frustration evident in his voice. "But in his mind, I'm the enemy. We need to be careful, Elena. Very careful."

Together, they tried to piece together a plan, realizing that their journey at Stanford was going to be fraught with more challenges than they'd ever imagined. Aarav paced the room for a few minutes, thinking, his brow furrowed in concentration. Elena watched him, hoping he would come up with something, anything, to quell the storm that had suddenly upended their lives.

Finally, he stopped and faced her. "Alright, Elena, I've been thinking. This may sound a bit wild, but bear with me."

Elena took a deep breath, bracing herself. "Okay, shoot."

He started, "In international relations, there's a concept called 'Soft Power.' Instead of using force, or hard power, nations use culture, political values, and foreign policies to influence others. It's a subtle approach, influencing without forcing."

Elena nodded, "I remember reading about it. But how does it apply here?"

"Well," Aarav continued, "we need to apply a similar strategy. Instead of confronting this directly, we can use our influence and skills to navigate this situation from the shadows. We'll gather intelligence, understand our enemy, and subtly push back without exposing ourselves."

Elena looked skeptical. "But why can't we just go to the police? This is a serious threat!"

Aarav sighed, "That's where it gets tricky. Being international students, we're on F-1 visas. Any legal entanglement could jeopardize our immigration status, even potentially leading to our visas being revoked. Not to mention the scholarship we're on. We're walking on a tightrope here. One false move, and everything we've worked for could crumble."

Elena shuddered at the thought. "Okay, so what's the plan?"

Aarav began to explain, "Firstly, we need to gather as much data as possible. I can trace the origins of the messages, maybe find out if others are being targeted, or if this is a larger scam. Then, using our knowledge of international relations, we can decipher any hidden meanings or patterns in the messages. Maybe they're using specific terminology or codes we can pick up on."

Elena chimed in, "We can also talk to some of the seniors in our program. They might have insights or advice. Stanford's a close-knit community. Someone might know something."

Aarav nodded, "Exactly. We approach this diplomatically. Gather allies, collect intelligence, and subtly push back. Soft power."

Elena took a deep breath, "Alright. Let's do this. But promise me one thing?"

Aarav looked at her, "Anything."

"We watch each other's backs. No solo missions."

Aarav smiled, pulling her into a reassuring hug, "Deal. Together, always."

With a plan in place and their determination renewed, Aarav and Elena set forth on their mission, ready to tackle the shadows that threatened to mar their bright future at Stanford.

* * * * *

New Beginnings and Looming Shadows

Elena, bleary-eyed from the early morning sunlight filtering through her window, squinted at the bouquet on her doorstep. The mix of vibrant tulips and roses brought a warm smile to her face. She bent down to pick them up, inhaling their sweet scent, her heart feeling lighter than it had in days. Attached to the bouquet was a small note. She unfolded it, reading Aarav's familiar handwriting.

"For a new beginning. All the best for your first day,

xoxo – Aarav"

Elena clutched the note to her chest for a moment, feeling grateful for this gesture. Aarav's thoughtfulness never ceased to amaze her. Even with the shadows of the past looming, and the threats they faced, he always found a way to bring light into their lives.

Refreshed and with a spring in her step, Elena prepared for her first day. She chose a light blue shirt paired with a pencil skirt, wanting to strike the right balance between professional and approachable. With the flowers in a vase on her table and the note pinned to her board, she headed out.

The campus was buzzing with energy. Freshmen were scattered around, trying to find their way, while the seniors moved with a familiar ease. Elena took a moment to breathe in the air, the scent of blooming flowers and fresh-cut grass, the underlying electric charge of excitement and anticipation.

She reached the International Relations building, a majestic structure with tall windows and grand arches, representing the legacy and prestige of Stanford. As she entered, she was greeted by Professor Mireille, the head of the department and also Elena's guide for her research assistant role.

"Ah, Ms. Elena! Welcome! I've heard so much about you. I'm thrilled to have you on board," Professor Mireille exclaimed, her enthusiasm contagious.

"Thank you, Professor. I'm eager to contribute and learn from this opportunity," Elena replied, shaking the professor's extended hand.

The day was a whirlwind of introductions, orientations, and planning sessions. Elena met the team she would be working with, a diverse group from different parts of the world, each bringing unique perspectives to the table.

As the day came to a close, and the amber hue of dusk began to cast its glow on Stanford, Elena felt content. The threats and shadows felt distant, at least for now. Today was about new beginnings and the promise of a brighter future.

She made her way back to her dorm, mentally replaying the day, and looking forward to sharing every detail with Aarav. The bouquet's fragrance filled her room, a silent testament to the bond they shared and the journey they were on together.

Aarav's POV

The soft light of dawn painted Aarav's room in muted hues of orange and pink. His sheets were tangled, evidence of a restless night. The weight of responsibility and the looming threat from Farhaan had kept him awake. Elena's safety was paramount to him, and the thought of any harm coming to her was unbearable.

Pushing away the blankets, Aarav sat up, rubbing the fatigue from his eyes. The stillness of the early morning was comforting, but his mind continued its relentless churn. He knew that he had to keep a clear head and remain proactive.

With that thought, Aarav decided to start his day with a jog. Stanford's campus was vast and picturesque, a mix of historic architecture and lush green spaces. The early morning was the perfect time to explore it, with the world still half-asleep and the pathways relatively empty.

As he ran, the rhythm of his footsteps combined with the steady beat of his heart, helping him clear his mind. The towering palm trees and the subtle scent of eucalyptus invigorated him, reminding him of the beauty of life and the importance of the present.

After a good thirty-minute run, Aarav returned to his dorm, feeling more centered. The physical exertion had pushed away some of the anxiety, and he felt ready to face the day.

He took a refreshing shower and dressed in his usual style – a crisp white shirt, dark jeans, and his favorite leather boots. Glancing at the mirror, he ran a hand through his hair, the slight wave giving it a casual flair.

Before leaving for his class, Aarav paused for a moment, his thoughts going to Elena. He remembered the vulnerability in her eyes, the fears they hadn't voiced. He decided to send her a small gesture to brighten her day – a bouquet of flowers.

With his day planned out and his mind set on his goals, Aarav walked to his first class, armed with determination and hope. Every step he took was a commitment – to Elena, to their love, and to overcoming the challenges that lay ahead.

The sun was high in the sky when Aarav made his way to the campus cafeteria. His morning had been hectic, filled with lectures, group discussions, and brainstorming sessions. But as the clock neared lunchtime, his thoughts drifted to Elena and their planned meetup.

As he entered the bustling cafeteria, he immediately spotted Elena at their usual corner table, deeply engrossed in a conversation with a few classmates. The way her eyes lit up with passion, her animated gestures, and the fluidity with which she presented her arguments, Aarav couldn't help but be captivated. He paused for a moment, just observing her, thinking about how she had grown and matured in the short time since they had arrived at Stanford.

Approaching the table, he heard snippets of their discussion — geopolitics, trade relations, and the implications of emerging global trends. Aarav was well-versed in these topics, given his interest in international relations, but hearing Elena discuss them with such depth and nuance filled him with pride. And he wasn't the only one impressed; her peers seemed to hang onto every word, nodding in agreement and occasionally interjecting with their own insights.

Aarav cleared his throat playfully, signaling his arrival. Elena looked up, her face breaking into a warm smile. "Hey there," she greeted, wrapping up her discussion with her peers.

As they excused themselves, Aarav took a seat across from Elena. "You seemed pretty engrossed. Anything interesting?"

Elena chuckled, pushing a stray strand of hair behind her ear. "Just discussing potential implications of the recent trade agreements. You know, the usual."

He leaned forward, smirking. "I must say, watching you talk research is... hot."

She laughed, her eyes sparkling with mischief. "Oh, is it? Maybe I should do it more often then."

Their playful banter continued as they shared their meal. The cafeteria's hustle and bustle faded into the background, leaving just the two of them in their bubble of shared understanding and love.

The rest of the afternoon flew by as they discussed everything from their coursework to future plans. As the shadows lengthened and the sun began to dip below the horizon, they reluctantly parted ways, each heading to their respective commitments.

But as they went their separate ways, they both carried with them the warmth of their bond, a love that seemed to grow stronger with each passing day.

At the end of their day, Elena and Aarav found a secluded bench on the main quad of Stanford's campus. The sun had dipped below the horizon, casting the area in a soft, golden hue. Students lounged on the grass, engaged in chatter or focused on their books.

Aarav looked around, ensuring no one was within earshot, before turning to Elena. "I think I have a plan."

Elena leaned in closer, her heart racing with a mix of anticipation and anxiety. "Tell me."

Aarav took a deep breath, his demeanor serious. "I found out that Farhan is here on an expired student visa. He overstayed after dropping out of his program two years ago."

Elena's eyes widened in surprise. "How did you find out?"

Aarav grinned, a hint of pride evident in his eyes. "Ethical hacking and some deep digging on the dark web. Took me a while, but I got there."

Elena was momentarily taken aback by Aarav's skills. "That's... impressive. And risky. But what's the plan?"

"We're not going to the local police," Aarav started, anticipating Elena's initial thought. "As we discussed, that could lead to unnecessary complications for us. But, given Farhan's immigration status, we can report him to the Immigration and Customs Enforcement (ICE)."

Elena frowned, processing this. "That could lead to his deportation."

Aarav nodded. "Exactly. It's a severe consequence, but he's threatened you, Elena. And he's operating here illegally. This might be the best way to ensure our safety without directly confronting him."

Elena pondered for a moment. The thought of causing someone's deportation weighed heavily on her, but she also recognized the threat Farhan posed. "Okay," she whispered, "we'll do it. But we have to be sure it's the right thing."

Aarav took Elena's hand, intertwining their fingers. "I believe it is, Elena. I want to protect you, protect us. But I also don't want to act without your agreement."

Elena leaned her head on Aarav's shoulder. "I trust you, Aarav. Let's do this together."

The pair sat there for a while, drawing strength from each other's presence, ready to face whatever challenges lay ahead.

* * * * *

In the Shadow of Decisions and Daggers

The following morning was unusually overcast for California. Heavy gray clouds blanketed the sky, a somber reflection of the task ahead. As Aarav laced up his running shoes, he took a moment to stare out his dorm window. The usual sunrise that greeted him with its golden embrace was absent, replaced by a muted, almost sorrowful light.

Taking a deep breath, Aarav started his run, using the rhythmic pounding of his feet against the pavement to clear his mind. The weight of the decision pressed on him, making each step feel slightly heavier than usual. He thought of Elena and the threat that loomed over them. As he sprinted, he mentally rehearsed the steps they would take later that day.

Finishing his run, Aarav headed to the campus shower facilities. The warm water cascaded down, washing away the sweat but not the nagging uncertainty. Dressed and ready, he checked his phone, noticing a text from Elena.

"Morning! How was your run? Meet at Coupa Café after our morning lectures?"

Aarav quickly responded, *"Sounds good. See you then."*

The morning passed in a blur, with Aarav's focus intermittently shifting between his lectures and their impending report on Farhan. The weight of their decision, the potential consequences, and the unknown aftermath raced through his mind.

By the time he reached Coupa Café, Elena was already there, nursing a cup of coffee, her laptop open in front of her. She looked up and offered him a faint smile. "Hey," she said softly.

"Hey," Aarav replied, taking the seat opposite her. "How are you holding up?"

Elena exhaled deeply. "Anxious, to be honest. But I know we're doing this for the right reasons."

Aarav nodded, placing a reassuring hand over hers. "We'll get through this together."

They spent the next hour discussing their courses, trying to distract themselves from the weighty task at hand. But as the clock ticked closer to the time they'd set for reporting Farhan, the atmosphere between them grew tense.

Finally, Elena closed her laptop, her eyes meeting Aarav's. "Are we really doing this?"

Aarav nodded firmly. "We are. And we'll face whatever comes next, together."

Taking a deep breath, the two of them left the café, hand in hand, ready to confront the shadows of their past and secure their future.

The path to the ICE was a familiar one, the worn cobblestones echoing the many footsteps of students over the years. The atmosphere, however, felt different today. Every rustling leaf, every cawing bird, and every passing shadow seemed to take on an ominous undertone.

They walked in silence, their hands tightly intertwined, each lost in their thoughts. Aarav's senses were on high alert. The heaviness in the air felt almost palpable. As they neared an alleyway, he sensed a sudden movement behind them.

Whipping around, Aarav's eyes met those of a hooded figure, eyes cold and filled with malice. Time seemed to slow as the glint of a blade caught the muted sunlight. Without a second thought, Aarav pushed Elena out of the way, positioning himself between her and their attacker. The sharp pain of the blade plunging into him brought everything into sharp focus.

Elena screamed, her voice echoing off the walls of the surrounding buildings. Farhaan, momentarily taken aback by the turn of events, started to retreat but not before pulling the blade out and leaving Aarav bleeding profusely.

Elena, panic-stricken, dropped to her knees beside Aarav, pressing her hands over his wound in a futile attempt to stem the flow of blood. Tears streamed down her face as she screamed for help.

Several students, hearing the commotion, rushed over. One quickly dialed 911, while others tried to provide some first aid.

"Stay with me, Aarav. Please, stay with me," Elena sobbed, holding onto him tightly.

Aarav, his face pale and lips quivering, managed a weak smile. "Always, Lena," he whispered, his voice strained.

The world seemed to blur around Elena as she trailed behind the ambulance. The deafening wail of the sirens seemed a distant echo compared to the pounding of her heart. Each red traffic light felt like a malevolent entity, conspiring to delay the crucial seconds that stood between life and death.

She had seen this scene play out in movies, read about it in novels — the desperate rush to the hospital, the anguish of uncertainty. But living it was a different kind of agony altogether. The fictional tales had always seemed dramatic; yet now, in the throes of real-life trauma, she wished she could say it was exaggerated.

The streets of the city flew by, but to Elena, every storefront, every face, and every car looked distorted — as if she was seeing them through a nightmarish lens. Time became elastic, stretching and compressing unpredictably. Moments felt like hours, and yet the entire journey seemed to pass in a blink.

She remembered a quote from Shakespeare's Macbeth, something she had analyzed in one of her literature classes: "Come, seeling night, scarf up the tender eye of pitiful day." Today, the day was indeed pitiful, its very light appearing to mock her anguish. The universe had chosen this day, of all days, to let the worst imaginable thing happen.

His image kept playing in her mind: Aarav, with that selfless and determined look on his face, the split-second decision he made, and the brutal aftermath. She felt a sinking feeling, thinking of how much blood he'd lost, a crimson stream that seemed endless on that cold cobblestone pathway.

By the time the ambulance screeched to a halt in front of the hospital, Elena felt numb. Nurses and doctors rushed out, seamlessly transferring Aarav into the emergency room. One nurse, seeing the sheer terror in Elena's eyes, gently guided her to a waiting area, urging her to sit.

But all Elena could think was how life, in its cruel unpredictability, had brought them to this moment. How just a few hours ago, they were discussing dreams, future plans, and now, they were here, teetering on the precipice of their worst nightmare.

Moments later, the wailing of sirens could be heard. Paramedics rushed over, efficiently taking over from the well-meaning students. They worked quickly, stabilizing Aarav as best as they could before lifting him onto a stretcher.

Elena, still in shock, was led away by a kind police officer who tried to comfort her, assuring her that they would do everything they could to catch Farhaan.

As the ambulance sped away, its lights flashing and sirens wailing, the gravity of the situation began to sink in for Elena. The man she loved had just risked his life to save hers. The weight of their love and the lengths to which they'd go to protect each other became painfully clear.

After 12 hours

Through the veil of pain and medication, Aarav's vision was foggy, but there was one unmistakable sight that grounded him — Elena. Her usually bright and sparkly eyes were swollen from crying, her face ashen with exhaustion. Yet, in that moment of raw vulnerability, he thought she looked more beautiful than ever.

With great effort, he managed to whisper her name, "Elena..." The sound, weak and raspy, seemed to electrify her. She bolted upright, her tear-filled eyes meeting his.

"Aarav?" she said in disbelief. Every emotion — relief, love, pain — was evident in her voice.

He tried to smile, to reassure her, but his body was still rebelling against him, making even the smallest movement feel like a monumental task. "Hey," he murmured.

Elena held his hand gently, her fingers trembling. "Don't you ever scare me like that again," she choked out between sobs.

"I'm sorry," he whispered, tears forming in his own eyes. The sheer gravity of what he had been through — and what he had put Elena through — began to weigh on him.

She leaned in, resting her forehead against his, and for a moment, they just breathed together, finding solace in each other's presence. It was a silent promise between them — a promise of facing whatever came their way, together.

The room was filled with the muted beeps of medical equipment and the soft glow of ambient lighting, but in that shared silence, the world outside ceased to exist. It was just

Aarav and Elena, connected by an unbreakable bond of love and shared adversity.

As the silence stretched between Aarav and Elena, he leaned in, capturing her lips in a tender kiss. It was a reaffirmation of their shared journey and love, their commitment to the path ahead.

The moment was broken by the soft sound of the door opening. Both of them turned to see a tall, well-dressed man with a stern face standing at the entrance. Aarav's father. The air in the room grew palpable, tension radiating from every corner.

Without waiting for an invitation, he strode in, his eyes taking in Elena briefly before settling on his injured son.

"Aarav," he began in a voice that carried authority, "I heard about the incident. I'm... glad you're okay."

The pause before 'glad' wasn't lost on Elena. She watched the interaction closely, seeing the deep-seated issues that lay beneath the surface of their relationship. Aarav responded with a nod, his expression hard to read.

His father continued, "I want you to remember the commitment you made, son. Our business needs you." He emphasized the word 'our,' as if trying to reiterate a shared destiny.

Elena's eyebrows furrowed slightly, her protective instincts flaring. She didn't like the undertone of the conversation, the pressure it seemed to put on Aarav when he was already vulnerable. But she held her tongue, knowing it wasn't her place to intervene.

Breaking the tension, Aarav's father reached into his coat pocket and produced a set of car keys. "Consider this a gift," he said, placing them on the bedside table. "A Tesla. It's parked outside the hospital."

Elena's eyes widened in surprise. She didn't knew Aarav came from a wealthy family, but the extent of their wealth and influence was slowly becoming clear.

"Do well, Aarav," his father added with a slight nod, "And remember our agreement." With that, he turned and walked out, leaving a trail of unsaid words and unexpressed emotions in his wake.

Aarav let out a sigh, closing his eyes briefly. Elena moved closer, her hand finding his. "A Tesla?" she whispered, trying to infuse a bit of lightness into the situation.

He managed a weak smile. "Yeah. His way of saying he cares, I guess."

Elena leaned in, kissing his forehead. "We'll figure everything out, okay? One step at a time."

He squeezed her hand in response, grateful for her unwavering support. Whatever the future held, they would face it together.

Farhaan's arrest was swift. The anonymous tip that Aarav and Elena had initially planned to drop, coupled with the evidence from the assault, left no room for him to wiggle out of the situation. Stanford's campus buzzed with the news, shockwaves reverberating through the student body. Nobody had imagined that beneath the facade of the charming student, there lay a dangerous threat.

The police, in collaboration with Stanford's internal security, acted promptly. It was revealed that Farhaan had multiple offenses back in his home country, including cyber threats and stalking. The US immigration department was now looking into his case, and it was very likely he would be deported after serving his jail sentence.

Aarav and Elena followed the news closely, mostly from the confines of Aarav's hospital room. The Stanford community rallied around them, with friends and strangers alike dropping by to offer their support.

Late one evening, after another long day, Elena lay beside Aarav on the hospital bed. The room was dimly lit, the soft hum of medical equipment offering a comforting background noise. Aarav's steady breathing signaled his descent into sleep, but Elena lay awake, her thoughts a jumbled mess.

She replayed the events of the past few days, grateful for the closure but still haunted by the threats and the danger they had faced. More than anything, she was curious about the mysterious agreement between Aarav and his father. The way his father had behaved, the gift of the Tesla, the emphasized reminder of their deal—it all hinted at something deeper, something she wasn't privy to.

She wanted to ask, to understand, but the timing never seemed right. Aarav had been through so much, and Elena didn't want to burden him further.

Feeling his warmth next to her, she was reminded of the strength of their bond. She knew that when the time was right, they would discuss everything. Until then, all that mattered was that they were together and safe.

Softly brushing Aarav's hair from his forehead, she leaned in and planted a gentle kiss. With that, she snuggled closer to him and allowed herself to drift into a peaceful sleep. The world outside could wait; for now, they had each other.

A months later

The soft morning sun filtered through the curtains, casting a warm glow over the room. The beeping of the hospital machines had been replaced by the chirping of birds and distant sounds of a bustling university campus. Aarav stretched languidly, the pain from his wound now a dull ache. Today was the day he'd finally be discharged.

Elena sat on the edge of the bed, scrolling through her phone, probably checking emails or catching up on the classwork they'd missed. She looked up and flashed Aarav a radiant smile, her eyes shining brighter than any morning sun.

"Ready to leave this place?" she asked, enthusiasm evident in her voice.

"You have no idea," he replied with a chuckle, slowly sitting up.

The process of discharge was fairly smooth. As they waited for the paperwork, Elena shared some of the more lighthearted news from the campus. Apparently, in their absence, a raccoon had gained notoriety for stealing food from the student canteen.

Aarav laughed, "Only at Stanford, right?"

Elena playfully nudged him, "Don't underestimate raccoons; they're clever little creatures."

Stepping out of the hospital, the fresh air felt rejuvenating. The world seemed brighter, more vibrant, and full of promise. With Elena by his side, Aarav felt invincible, ready to face any challenge.

They decided to take things slow for the first few days. A mix of relaxed brunches, movie marathons in bed, and long walks around the campus. It was like they were rediscovering Stanford, seeing it with fresh eyes.

One evening, as they lay on the grass looking up at the stars, Aarav spoke, "You know, this whole ordeal has made me realize how fleeting life can be. We should cherish every moment."

Elena nodded, squeezing his hand, "It's taught me the importance of being with the right people. The ones who stand by you, no matter what."

They spent a lot of time discussing their future, their dreams, and aspirations. Both were ambitious, and Stanford was just the beginning. Aarav wanted to delve deep into international relations, hoping to make a mark in diplomacy. Elena, on the other hand, was keen on research, wanting to influence global policies through her work.

Life had thrown them a curveball, but it had only strengthened their resolve. As the days turned into weeks, the traumatic memories began to fade, replaced by hopeful plans and shared laughter.

Their bond grew deeper, their love more profound. They were not just partners in love but in life's journey, guiding and supporting each other through the highs and lows. And as Stanford's sprawling campus witnessed their love story unfold, it was evident that no challenge was insurmountable for Aarav and Elena, as long as they faced it together.

The trees of Stanford's Main Quad had seen countless students pass under their shade, each with dreams in their eyes and ambition in their hearts. But this year, the historic walls and pathways bore witness to the resilience and determination of Aarav and Elena.

The academic year was a whirlwind of lectures, seminars, research, and late-night study sessions. There were times when the weight of their coursework seemed unbearable. But the memories of their shared trials and tribulations, of the challenges they had already faced and overcome together, gave them the strength to persevere.

Elena, with her sharp analytical skills, excelled in her research assignments. She soon became a favorite of her professors, and her articles started getting recognition in esteemed journals. Aarav, with his eloquent speeches and vast knowledge, dominated the MUNs and debates, earning accolades and respect from his peers.

As the final exams approached, the pressure intensified. The library became their second home, with endless cups of coffee and stacks of reference books surrounding them. They would often quiz each other, trying to make the revision process as interactive as possible. On particularly challenging nights, Aarav would recount funny anecdotes from their past or hum a soothing tune to calm Elena's frazzled nerves.

The day the results were posted was one of nervous anticipation. Students gathered around the notice board, scanning for their names and grades. When Elena and Aarav finally saw their results, the relief and joy were palpable. Not only had they cleared all their exams, but they had also scored among the top of their class.

Elena hugged Aarav tightly, tears of happiness in her eyes. "We did it," she whispered.

Aarav, lifting her chin to meet his gaze, said, "No, *we* did it. **Together.**"

That evening, the duo celebrated with their friends at a local diner. The air was filled with laughter, music, and the clinking of glasses. As they relished their favorite dishes and recounted the ups and downs of the year, it was clear that the trials they faced had only made their bond stronger.

Late into the night, as they walked back to their dorms, Aarav paused and looked at the starry sky. "You know, this year taught us that we can face anything as long as we're together."

Elena nodded, wrapping her arm around his waist. "Here's to many more years of milestones and memories."

And as they walked hand in hand, the Stanford arches stood tall and proud, a silent testament to their journey and the many more adventures that awaited them.

The air had grown cooler as the night deepened. The campus, bathed in the soft glow of streetlights, was serene and peaceful. Aarav glanced at his watch and a knowing smile played on his lips. Elena, lost in the beauty of the moment, didn't notice as he subtly reached into his backpack.

As the clock tower echoed the twelve chimes, Aarav gently tapped Elena's shoulder, making her turn. "Happy birthday, Elena," he whispered, his eyes shimmering with mischief and warmth.

She blinked in surprise, having momentarily forgotten the significance of the date amidst the whirlwind of exams and celebrations. "Thank you," she managed to say, her voice filled with emotion.

But before she could say more, Aarav handed her a beautifully wrapped box. The packaging was simple, yet elegant. "I hope you like it," he said with a hint of nervousness.

Elena slowly unwrapped the gift, revealing a leather-bound journal. Its pages were made of handmade paper, and the cover was embossed with intricate designs. Tucked inside the journal was a delicate silver pen. But what truly caught her attention was a handwritten note on the first page.

"To Elena,

May you fill these pages with your dreams, thoughts, and the stories of our shared adventures. Every day with you feels like a new chapter, and I'm grateful for every moment. Here's to writing our story together.

Always,

Aarav."

Tears welled up in Elena's eyes as she looked up at Aarav. "This is beautiful," she whispered. "Thank you for always understanding me. I've always wanted to document our journey, and this... this is perfect."

Aarav smiled, pulling her into a warm embrace. "Happy birthday, Elena. Here's to more dreams, more adventures, and more memories."

And under the canopy of stars, with the world around them asleep, they shared a quiet moment, holding onto the promise of many more shared tomorrows.

* * * * *

Sunset and Sunrises, Ties That Bind

The campus was unusually quiet, with most of the students having gone home for the vacation. Stanford's magnificent architecture, which was always bustling with activity, seemed to have taken a break too, giving the landscape an almost surreal serenity. Elena and Aarav had chosen to stay back, partly because of their commitments and partly because they both found solace in each other's company.

One evening, as they sat on a blanket in the university's main quad, with soft jazz playing in the background from a portable speaker, Elena finally mustered the courage to ask a question that had been bothering her for some time.

"Aarav," she began hesitantly, "about that day in the hospital... when your father visited. What was that agreement he mentioned?"

Aarav's face grew slightly tense. He'd hoped to keep that part of his life separate from the world he'd built with Elena. Taking a deep breath, he replied, "It's nothing, Elena. Just a family matter."

She looked into his eyes, searching for answers. "It seemed important. I could see it in both of your eyes. Is it something to do with his business?"

Aarav sighed. "I promised him that I'd take over the family business once I was done with my studies here. But that's still some time away. And I made that promise under... different circumstances."

"But why? Is that what you want? To run his business?" Elena's voice held a mixture of concern and curiosity.

He paused, choosing his words carefully. "It's not about what I want, Elena. Sometimes, we make choices for the greater good. It's complicated."

She reached out, taking his hand. "Aarav, you've always told me to follow my heart, to chase my dreams. You deserve the same. If there's anything bothering you, please share it with me. We're in this together, remember?"

Aarav looked at their intertwined hands and then into Elena's earnest eyes. "It's just... I've seen the weight my father carries, managing the business, handling the responsibility. And with everything that happened... I just felt it was my duty to step in."

"But at the cost of your dreams?" Elena pressed gently.

Aarav hesitated, then whispered, "Maybe it's time I figured out what my dreams truly are."

The evening sun cast a golden hue on the campus as the two sat there, lost in their thoughts, drawing strength from each other.

As Elena stared at her phone screen, her fingers trembling, the color drained from her face. "Abuela?" she whispered, her voice barely audible.

"Elena," came the frail voice of her grandmother, "mi niña, I just wanted to hear your voice one more time."

Tears welled up in Elena's eyes. "Abuela, please don't say that. You're strong, you'll pull through."

The elderly voice on the other end sounded tired but full of love. "I've lived a long life, Elena. But my time is drawing near. I just wanted to tell you how proud I am of you."

Before Elena could reply, her cousin Rafael took the phone. "Elena," he said, his voice thick with emotion, "you should come home. Abuela wants to see you."

Nodding, even though she knew Rafael couldn't see her, Elena managed to reply, "I'll be there as soon as I can."

Aarav, sensing the gravity of the situation, had already started searching for the earliest flights to Mexico. Wrapping an arm around Elena, he whispered reassuringly, "I've got you. We'll get you home."

By dawn, they were on their way to the airport, the weight of the situation pressing heavily on their hearts. Aarav held Elena's hand throughout the flight, offering silent support.

They arrived in Elena's hometown by midday. The warm Mexican sun and the familiar scent of home were both comforting and heart-wrenching for Elena. As they approached her family's house, she could see relatives gathered, their faces a mix of sadness and hope.

Rafael greeted them at the door, his eyes red from crying. He hugged Elena tightly and gave a nod of acknowledgment to Aarav. "Thank you for bringing her home," he whispered to Aarav.

Elena's reunion with her grandmother was bittersweet. Abuela, though frail and weak, lit up at the sight of her beloved granddaughter. They shared tender moments, reminiscing about the past and speaking of love and life.

As the days passed, the inevitable came. Surrounded by family and loved ones, Abuela took her final breath, leaving behind a legacy of love and memories.

Aarav, though an outsider to the family, was Elena's pillar of strength throughout. He supported her, comforted her, and ensured she had everything she needed.

In the midst of grief and loss, Elena found solace in Aarav's unwavering presence. They had faced numerous challenges in their journey together, but this experience, in particular, deepened their bond and commitment to each other.

* * * * *

A LOVE TESTED

Stanford's sprawling campus was bathed in the soft, amber hues of autumn. But for Elena, the world seemed gray and distant. The echoing laughter and vibrant conversations around her seemed from another world, a world she once was a part of.

Aarav watched with a heavy heart as Elena immersed herself in her research, trying to escape her grief. The once lively girl, full of dreams and ambitions, now spent long hours in the library, drowning in books and papers. Every time he tried to pull her out, to remind her of the world outside, she would retreat further into her shell.

He understood her pain; the loss of a loved one was devastating. But he also feared for her well-being. The balance between work and life had tilted dangerously, and Elena's health was at stake.

One evening, Aarav found Elena in the library, her face buried in a pile of books, her eyes red from crying. He sat down next to her, gently took her hand, and said, "Elena, I know how much Abuela meant to you. And I understand that this is your way of coping. But you're hurting yourself.

You need to grieve, to process, to heal. This...this isn't the way."

Elena looked up, her eyes brimming with tears. "I just...I miss her so much, Aarav. And the work, it helps... it helps me forget."

He squeezed her hand, "I'm here for you, Elena. Always. But this isn't about forgetting. It's about remembering, cherishing, and moving forward. We'll get through this together."

In the gentle hush of twilight, Aarav led Elena to his dorm room, their fingers interwined, a silent promise exchanged through a glance. The room was dim, lit only by the soft glow of a single lamp, casting elongated shadows that danced upon the walls.

He pulled her close, and in that moment, there was an electricity in the air, reminiscent of Taylor Swift's lyrics - a mix of yearning and anticipation. "*This night is sparkling, don't you let it go, I'm wonderstruck, blushing all the way home.*"

Their lips met, a delicate touch at first, then with growing passion. The world outside ceased to exist, as the rhythm of their heartbeats merged into a harmonious symphony. Their breaths mingled, warmth spreading like wildfire, leaving a trail of burning desire.

Elena's fingers traced the contours of Aarav's face, down to the nape of his neck, sending shivers down his spine. Aarav gently brushed the tresses from her face, revealing the intensity of her gaze, echoing the lyrics, "*I was enchanted to meet you.*"

Their clothes seemed like barriers, and as layers peeled away, they found solace in the heat of each other's embrace. Time seemed to stop, every touch a lyric, every sigh a melody. It was an exploration, a celebration of love and intimacy. The world outside their room blurred, as they lost themselves in the depths of passion.

As dawn's first light crept into the room, they lay wrapped in each other's arms, bodies entwined, souls connected. A silent promise made, a journey begun. For in that night, they hadn't just made love; they had written a poetic chapter of their shared story.

As the golden fingers of dawn stretched into the room, they basked in its warmth, their bodies cocooned in a tapestry of sheets and bare skin. Elena nestled her head on Aarav's chest, listening to the rhythmic beating of his heart – a lullaby in its own right.

For a long time, neither spoke, as if fearing that words might fracture the delicate magic of the moment. But then, Aarav began to talk, his voice soft, almost a whisper, opening up about the memories that haunted him, the shadows of his past. He spoke of his childhood, of the love he once held for his father, now tarnished by the weight of betrayal and the pain of unfulfilled expectations.

Elena listened intently, her fingers tracing idle patterns on Aarav's arm. And as he revealed his vulnerabilities, she found the courage to share her own. She spoke of the warmth of her abuela's embrace, the life lessons taught in the small kitchen of their home in Mexico, and the piercing void left behind after her passing. She revealed the weight of carrying on her family's legacy, the challenge of blending traditions with modern aspirations.

They laughed at shared follies from their teenage years and mused over dreams they had yet to chase. They delved into the complexities of relationships, the sting of heartbreaks past, and the hope for future love.

By the time the sun was fully up, painting the room with its golden hue, they had traversed the landscapes of their lives, discovering new facets of each other. Vulnerabilities were laid bare, and in doing so, they found strength in their bond. They realized that love wasn't just about sharing moments of passion but also about embracing each other's scars and healing together.

The room was filled with a profound intimacy, transcending the physical realm. And as they drifted into a contented sleep, curled up together, they were more connected than ever. The walls that had once stood between them had crumbled, making way for a love that was deep, unyielding, and true.

The peaceful morning was broken by the shrill tone of Aarav's phone, its urgency shattering the tranquil bubble the two had enveloped themselves in. With a sigh, Aarav reached out and took the call. His face, which moments ago held a soft, contented glow, shifted rapidly through a series of emotions: surprise, confusion, anger, and finally, a deep-seated dread.

Elena, sensing the sudden tension in the room, sat up and watched him intently. "What is it?" she whispered, her voice filled with concern.

"It's... It's about the business," Aarav said, his voice barely audible. "Something's happened. Something big."

As Elena tried to probe further, Aarav's phone buzzed again, this time displaying a series of alarming news alerts. The headlines blared out: "Major Financial Scandal Rocks Global Markets!" and right there, in bold letters, was the name of Aarav's family business.

Aarav's breath caught in his throat. The world he had left behind, the responsibilities he had tried to escape, were now catching up with him, threatening to tear apart the life he had begun to build at Stanford.

The promise he had made to his father, the reluctant agreement to take over the business, all of it came flooding back. The sanctuary that Stanford had become for him, the love he had found with Elena, now hung in the balance as the shadows of his family's legacy loomed large.

What had been a morning of connection and understanding was suddenly overshadowed by a crisis that threatened to redefine Aarav's future and test the strength of their bond. The next chapter in their journey had just begun, and it promised to be more challenging than anything they had faced before.

* * * * *

Part III

Chapter 20

Two Anchors in a Storm

Aarav sat on the edge of the bed, head in his hands, his usually calm demeanor now replaced by a facade of panic. Elena, her own worries momentarily pushed aside, approached him, trying to offer solace. “We can handle this,” she whispered, caressing his back.

Aarav glanced up at the myriad news notifications on his phone, each one more damning than the last. His family’s company, a pillar in the financial world for decades, had been implicated in a major scandal involving funds embezzlement and offshore accounts. The fallout was catastrophic, not just for the business, but for the family’s reputation.

“I have to go back,” Aarav muttered, the weight of responsibility pressing down on him. “I have to fix this, E.”

Elena’s heart ached seeing him like this. “And you will,” she responded firmly. “But you’re not alone in this. We’re in it together.”

Despite the situation's gravity, Aarav couldn't help but smile weakly. "I can't drag you into this mess."

"You aren't dragging me anywhere," she retorted. "I chose to be with you, through thick and thin. And right now, we'll face this storm together."

Determined, Aarav began making arrangements for an emergency trip home. He needed to confront his father, figure out the truth, and assess the damage. Elena, despite her own battles, decided she would accompany him.

However, before they could leave, an unexpected visitor arrived at Stanford. Raghav, Aarav's younger brother and a key figure in the family business, landed up at his dormitory.

"Big brother," Raghav greeted, his voice heavy with sarcasm. "Finally decided to come out of your ivory tower?"

Aarav's relationship with Raghav had always been complicated. Younger by just two years, Raghav had been thrust into the company's helm when Aarav chose a different path. The responsibility had been immense, and the resentment towards Aarav had only grown.

"I'm here to help," Aarav asserted.

Raghav sneered. "Oh, now you want to help? After all the damage's been done?"

Their argument escalated, echoing past wounds and unspoken grievances. Elena intervened, trying to mediate, but the tension was palpable. The brothers, once inseparable in childhood, now stood worlds apart.

Raghav leaned back in the chair, running a hand through his hair. He looked weary, the dark circles under his eyes testifying to sleepless nights. The room was silent for a moment, filled only with the distant hum of the Stanford campus outside.

"Raghav," Aarav began, trying to choose his words carefully, "Tell me everything."

Raghav's gaze hardened. "It began a few months ago. Anonymous tips sent to our competitors, leaking our business strategies, new ventures… everything."

Aarav frowned, "But how? We always ensured our data was secure."

"That's the baffling part," Raghav admitted. "It seems the leaks are coming from someone on the inside. Someone we trusted."

Elena, who had been quietly observing the exchange, interjected, "Have you identified any suspects?"

"We have a few in mind," Raghav responded tersely. "But the damage is done. The media's having a field day, and our stock prices have plummeted."

Aarav's eyes darted to his brother, "And Dad?"

Raghav hesitated, the weight of the situation evident on his face. "His health's deteriorated rapidly. The stress, the betrayal. And there are whispers that he might even be complicit, although I don't believe them for a second."

Elena could see the raw pain in Aarav's eyes. She reached out, taking his hand in hers, offering silent support.

"I need to see him," Aarav stated, his voice barely above a whisper.

"You will," Raghav said, the hardness in his voice melting for a moment. "But you should be prepared.

The father you remember and the man he's become... They're not the same."

Aarav nodded, determination setting in. "Then we'll face this together. We'll find the mole, clear our family's name, and rebuild."

Raghav looked skeptical. "And if it turns out that Dad is involved?"

Aarav's gaze was unwavering. "Then we'll deal with that when the time comes. But first, we need to understand the full extent of this mess."

The two brothers locked eyes, an unspoken understanding passing between them. Despite their differences and strained relationship, they were united in their desire to protect their family's legacy.

Elena squeezed Aarav's hand tighter. "We'll get through this. Together."

The storm was just beginning, but with resolve, unity, and love, they hoped to weather it.

* * * * *

The sleek lines of the private jet contrasted starkly with the turmoil that occupied Aarav's mind. The plush leather seats, the shining interiors, and the soft hum of the engines stood in stark contrast to the world outside.

Elena, unaccustomed to such opulence, took a moment to absorb her surroundings. She had always known about Aarav's affluent background, but it was another thing entirely to witness it firsthand. She hesitated for a split second before settling into a seat, feeling out of place amidst the luxury.

Aarav was lost in thought. Files, spreadsheets, emails – he was scouring through all the data available on the onboard computer. His fingers moved swiftly, his brow furrowed, seeking patterns, clues, inconsistencies; anything that might shed light on the identity of the traitor within.

Raghav, exhausted from the emotional and mental strain, reclined in a seat, eyes closed but mind undoubtedly racing. The tension in the aircraft was palpable, a silent testament to the storm brewing ahead.

Elena took out her laptop, immersing herself in her research. The stakes might be different, but the feeling of pursuit, of unraveling a mystery, resonated with her too. Every so often, she would glance at Aarav, admiring his determination and focus.

Hours passed. The sky outside transformed from a brilliant blue to shades of orange and red as the sun set. Elena felt a gentle tap on her shoulder. It was one of the onboard staff, offering refreshments.

She declined, her attention redirected to Aarav, who was still engrossed in his mission. Moving to his side, she gently placed a hand on his shoulder. He looked up, the weight of his worries evident in his gaze.

"Take a break," she whispered. "You can't solve everything in one go."

Aarav sighed, setting the tablet down. "I just feel so... powerless."

"You're doing everything you can," Elena assured him. "And I'm here with you, every step of the way."

For the first time since they boarded the jet, Aarav allowed himself a small smile. With Elena by his side, he felt fortified, ready to face whatever challenges lay ahead.

The plane touched down, signaling the beginning of their battle against the shadows threatening to engulf the legacy of the Mehta family.

The Mehta estate was a sprawling compound, surrounded by high walls and guards stationed at every corner. As they drove through the imposing gates, the opulence of the mansion came into full view. Glistening fountains, manicured gardens, and grandiose architecture; it was a symbol of power, wealth, and legacy.

But the regal exterior was marred by an unmistakable tension in the air. As they entered the mansion, they were greeted by a flurry of activity. Lawyers, board members, and family friends paced the corridors, engaged in hushed discussions.

At the heart of it all was Mr. Mehta, Aarav's father. Seated at his grand study, he looked older than Elena remembered from the photos she'd seen. The weight of the betrayal and the looming scandal had taken its toll.

Raghav stepped forward, introducing Elena. "Father, this is Elena, Aarav's friend from Stanford."

Mr. Mehta nodded, offering a weak smile. "Ah, I've heard much about you. Welcome to our home, though I wish it were under better circumstances."

Even though they already met at the hospital Aarav's father does not seem to remeber Elena

Elena nodded respectfully. "Thank you, sir."

Without wasting time, Aarav delved into the matter at hand. "Father, from what I've seen so far, the mole has left a trail. We can find them, but we need full access."

Mr. Mehta sighed, rubbing his temples. "Son, the board is in an uproar. They want answers, and they want them fast. Some even call for my resignation."

"We'll get those answers," Aarav said determinedly.

For days, the mansion became a war room. Documents were combed through, financial transactions traced, and employees interrogated. Elena, despite being an outsider, lent her analytical skills, drawing parallels from her studies in international relations. Betrayal, after all, was a universal theme.

One evening, as they pored over company emails, Elena stumbled upon a coded message. "Aarav," she said, excitement evident in her voice, "look at this. This doesn't belong in a financial report."

The message read: "*Rise of Phoenix imminent. Prepare for the new dawn.*"

Aarav's eyes widened. "Phoenix... That's a code name we'd joked about in college, referencing a hypothetical scenario where our business would be usurped."

It clicked. The mole was someone from Aarav's past, possibly even a close friend. But who? And why?

The weight of the revelation hung heavily between them. They had a lead, but it also meant confronting ghosts from Aarav's past. Would he be ready to face them?

As the night deepened, a storm raged outside, mirroring the tempest brewing within the walls of the Mehta estate. In the midst of the chaos, Aarav found solace only in Elena's presence. With every revelation and every challenge, she stood by him unwaveringly, a pillar of strength and support.

* * * * *

Late one evening, after another grueling session of piecing together the puzzle, Aarav pulled Elena aside into one of the mansion's balconies. The storm had subdued, leaving behind a gentle drizzle. The ambient sound of raindrops served as a soothing backdrop to their frayed nerves.

"Thank you," he whispered, brushing a stray strand of hair from Elena's face. "For being here. With me."

Elena looked up into Aarav's eyes, seeing a mix of vulnerability and determination. "You're not alone in this, Aarav. We're a team, remember?"

Aarav leaned in, capturing her lips in a soft, lingering kiss. The world around them blurred, and for that fleeting moment, there was no scandal, no betrayal—just them, finding solace in each other's embrace.

They stood like that for what felt like an eternity, wrapped up in one another, drawing strength and comfort. Elena finally broke the silence, her voice a gentle whisper. "Promise me something, Aarav."

"Anything."

"That no matter how deep we go into this mess, you won't let it consume you. Promise me that you'll always remember this moment, us, and what we mean to each other."

Aarav tightened his grip around her, pulling her close. "I promise," he murmured, sealing his vow with another gentle kiss.

In the familiar confines of his old room, a place filled with memories of a simpler time, Aarav gently took Elena's hand and led her inside. The air was thick with tension and anticipation. Both could sense the layers of emotions that had been building up, needing release.

The dim light from the bedside lamp painted a soft hue, lending an intimate atmosphere. Without a word, Aarav slowly started to unbutton his shirt, all the while holding Elena's gaze, seeking silent consent. With a nod, Elena mirrored his actions, revealing a vulnerability she had reserved just for him.

Aarav's fingers lightly traced the curve of her face, down her neck, and further, setting a trail of fire on her skin. They came closer, their lips meeting in a kiss that conveyed their pent-up emotions—a blend of fear, desperation, love, and longing. The world outside, with its problems and scandals, melted away.

The sounds of their mingled breaths, the rustling of sheets, and the whispered confessions of love filled the room. Each touch spoke volumes, a silent language that only the two of them understood. They explored and celebrated each other, finding ecstasy in the shared intimacy.

As dawn approached, they lay together, spent, nestled in each other's arms. The room, filled with their shared warmth, felt like a safe haven, sheltering them from the storm outside.

Elena murmured softly into Aarav's ear, her voice filled with emotion. "In this chaotic world, with you, I find peace."

Aarav tightened his embrace, kissing her forehead. "And with you, I find strength."

The outside world would soon beckon with its trials and tribulations, but in that moment, nothing else mattered. They had each other, and that was enough.

The sunlight filtered through the lace curtains, casting dappled shadows across the elegant dining room. The table was set with gleaming china, delicate silverware, and crystal glasses, reflecting the status and affluence of the family. The servants moved quietly, setting down dishes filled with sumptuous fare.

Aarav's mother entered the room, a picture of grace in her soft, pastel saree. Her demeanor was regal but the lines on her face told a tale of years of keeping secrets and bearing burdens. Raghav was already seated, looking weary but trying to keep up a cheerful front.

Aarav held out a chair for Elena, who hesitated for a second before taking her seat. The opulence was new to her, but she held herself with dignity, appreciating the stark contrast between her own upbringing and the life that Aarav had always known.

"Good morning, Amma," Aarav greeted, touching Meena's feet in a traditional sign of respect.

She smiled, her eyes misty. "It's good to have you home, beta."

Dinner commenced with light conversation. Meena, curious about Elena, initiated a conversation, "Elena, how did you find Stanford? It must be so different from Mexico."

Elena, with a bright smile, replied, "It is, Auntie. But it's a beautiful place. Both the campus and the community have been welcoming."

As the conversation flowed, Aarav couldn't help but notice the slight strain in the air. Raghav was quieter than usual, occasionally glancing at Aarav, as if trying to convey something unsaid.

After dessert was served, Meena excused herself, leaving the siblings and Elena alone. Raghav cleared his throat, "Aarav, we need to discuss the company's situation in detail. The board is panicking."

Elena, sensing the gravity, offered, "I can give you both some space to talk."

Aarav held her hand gently, "No. Stay. I want you here."

A deep dive into the company's affairs ensued. Documents were spread out on the table, figures discussed, and strategies pondered upon. Elena listened intently, occasionally asking questions, revealing her keen analytical mind.

Hours seemed to fly, and by the time they were wrapping up, night had fallen.

Raghav, rubbing his temples, sighed, "Thank you, Aarav, for stepping in. And Elena, thank you for your insights."

Elena smiled, "Anything for family."

Aarav's heart swelled with pride and love. In the midst of the storm, he realized he had two anchors – his love for Elena and his responsibility towards his family. The chapter ahead wouldn't be easy, but together, they would face whatever came their way.

* * * * *

THE DARKEST HOUR

Aarav and Elena spent the following days delving deeper into the company's intricacies. They went through contracts, deals, and correspondences in a bid to unearth the mole and any discrepancies.

One evening, as Elena was going through a pile of financial statements, she found an anomaly. "Aarav," she beckoned, "look at this."

He moved closer, his eyes scanning the figures she pointed to. "These transactions...they don't make sense. They're routed through an offshore account."

Elena nodded, "And look at the dates. All these transactions happened when major deals were signed."

Realization dawned upon Aarav. "These could be possible bribes or a way to siphon off funds. We need to trace this account."

Working late into the night, with their combined skills, they managed to trace the account to a shell company. "This is it, Elena. If we can link someone from our company to this shell company, we've got our mole."

The next day, Aarav confronted the board with his findings. Accusations flew, defenses were raised, but finally, under pressure, the mole was revealed – it was one of the senior managers who had been with the company for over a decade.

Aarav was filled with a mix of anger and betrayal, "Why? You were like family to us."

The manager looked down, shame evident on his face, "Greed, Aarav. Just greed. I thought I could get away with it."

With the mole exposed, Aarav and Raghav started the process of damage control. The days were grueling, filled with meetings with lawyers, PR teams, and stakeholders.

During a particularly stressful day, Aarav found respite in Elena. They walked in the gardens of the palatial home, hand in hand. Elena broke the silence, "Do you ever miss the simpler times, Aarav?"

He smiled, looking into the distance, "Every day. But this is my responsibility, and I need to set things right."

She nestled closer, "Remember, you're not alone in this."

Aarav pulled her close, his lips brushing her forehead, "I know. And that's what keeps me going."

* * * * *

The ambiance in the mansion was stifling, filled with tension. Aarav had always sensed something amiss, a jigsaw piece that just wouldn't fit. His research into the company, and the mole's confession, had only taken him so far. But the signs were there – things were just a little too convenient, the trails just a little too easy to follow.

Late one evening, as Aarav was going through some old photos, he noticed something. There were too many instances of Raghav and the now-exposed manager together – golf outings, parties, casual lunches. The kind of closeness that didn't come from just a professional relationship.

He confronted Raghav. "You were involved, weren't you?" His voice was a dangerous whisper.

Raghav scoffed, "Don't be foolish. Why would I sabotage our own company?"

But Aarav had seen through the charade, "It's always been about jealousy, hasn't it? Being born to a different mother, feeling second best..."

The room grew cold with Raghav's rage. "It was never about jealousy, Aarav. It was about fairness. You were always the golden child, the prince in waiting. I was pushed to the shadows, overlooked, and neglected. But I wanted to create something of my own, away from the shadow of our father and you."

Raghav's face contorted with fury and desperation, and in a swift move, he pulled out a gun. Elena, entering the room with a tray of coffee, froze in place. Time seemed to slow down.

Their father burst into the room, having overheard the confrontation. "Raghav, put the gun down!" he yelled, his voice filled with anguish.

For a few endless moments, the room was filled with tension so thick it could be cut with a knife. Then, with a cry of rage and despair, Raghav dropped the gun and sank to the ground, tears streaming down his face.

"I just wanted to be seen, to be recognized," he sobbed.

Their father approached Raghav, wrapping his arms around his distraught son. "I'm sorry," he whispered, tears in his eyes, "I'm so, so sorry."

The emotional tension in the room was palpable, tears still streaking the faces of the family members. Just when it seemed that the situation was de-escalating, Raghav's features twisted in fury once again. With a guttural scream, he lunged at Aarav with a concealed knife, aiming straight for his heart.

Aarav's reflexes, sharpened from years of sports and self-defense training, kicked in. He sidestepped, grabbed Raghav's arm, and, using his momentum, slammed him hard against the wall. There was a sickening crunch as the knife's blade, intended for Aarav, plunged into Raghav's own chest.

Everyone froze, stunned by the suddenness of the act. Raghav's face went pale, his eyes widening in shock. Blood seeped from the wound, staining his white shirt a dark, ominous red. He slid down the wall, life slipping from him.

"No!" their father cried, rushing to Raghav's side, cradling his dying son. "Raghav... please... hold on."

Elena, her face ashen, grabbed the house phone, dialing emergency services. But it was clear; it was too late. Raghav's eyes glazed over, and his body went limp.

Aarav sank to his knees, the weight of what he had done – in self-defense, yet so tragically fatal – crushing him. The grand room, which had witnessed countless happy family memories, was now the backdrop of an unthinkable fratricide.

"I didn't mean to... I didn't want this..." Aarav's voice broke, tears streaming down his face.

Elena rushed to his side, holding him close. "It was self-defense, Aarav. You didn't have a choice."

But the truth was, choices had been made long before this night — choices of favoritism, jealousy, and ambition. And now, they had culminated in a tragedy that would forever mark the family's legacy.

Sirens blared in the distance, growing louder and more foreboding with each passing second. The ancestral mansion, usually insulated from the outside world by its vast grounds, was now punctuated by the harsh flashing of blue and red lights.

Aarav, face stained with tears and drenched in a mix of sweat and disbelief, looked up to see a team of officers and medics burst into the room. Elena held his hand tightly, attempting to provide some semblance of comfort and security in the midst of chaos.

Before Aarav could speak, his father rose, a man once so towering and formidable, now seeming older, frailer. He locked eyes with the leading officer, his gaze steady but filled with unmistakable sorrow.

"It was me," he declared, his voice hoarse but firm. "I killed my son, Raghav, in self-defense."

Aarav's eyes widened in shock, his mouth opening to protest, but Elena's grip on his hand tightened, urging him to stay silent. His father's words hung heavily in the air, casting a shadow over the tragic scene. The officers exchanged glances, taking in the scene: the deceased, the bloodied knife, the family members in shock.

One of the officers, a stern-looking woman with graying hair, stepped forward. "You're confessing to the act?"

"Yes," Aarav's father responded, a single tear escaping his eye. "I never intended for any of this. I loved my son. But in a moment of self-preservation, I did the unthinkable."

Elena whispered into Aarav's ear, "He's protecting you."

Aarav nodded, his throat tight. He knew that his father, with all his influence and connections, stood a better chance in the labyrinth of the legal system than he did. Yet the magnitude of the sacrifice weighed heavily on him.

The officer signaled to her team. "Take him into custody."

As Aarav's father was led away, handcuffed, he glanced back at his surviving son, giving a reassuring nod. "Take care of everything, Aarav. Make it right."

Aarav nodded, tears streaming down. He knew that, in his father's eyes, this was a final act of redemption, an ultimate sacrifice for the son he had always favored. Yet the road ahead seemed daunting, filled with challenges and tribulations.

But for now, with Elena by his side, Aarav would find the strength to navigate the aftermath of the family's darkest hour.

* * * * *

Rising From the Ashes

The following week was a whirlwind for Aarav. Media outlets clamored for a statement from the new CEO of Mehta Enterprises, a company previously embroiled in scandal and now shaken by a family tragedy. Aarav faced them with grace and poise, answering questions with professionalism, managing to separate personal grief from his professional role.

The share market, sensing the stability Aarav brought to the table, responded positively. Mehta Enterprises stock prices stabilized and even began a slow ascent, a sign of confidence in the young CEO's capability.

Meanwhile, at Stanford, Elena worked diligently, sifting through the collective research she and Aarav had accumulated. With the data analyzed and compiled, she submitted their joint paper to one of the leading journals in international relations. Their groundbreaking findings, combined with the weight of Aarav's name, ensured that their work was received with considerable interest. Elena's dedication not only honored their combined efforts but also solidified her position as an emerging scholar in her field.

As weeks turned into months, Aarav's leadership proved transformative for Mehta Enterprises. Implementing innovative strategies, he streamlined operations, expanded into new markets, and fostered an inclusive work culture. The name "Aarav Mehta" became synonymous with business acumen and integrity, a brand in itself.

However, amidst board meetings, late-night negotiations, and global travels, Aarav's heart always sought solace in Elena. They maintained their bond through video calls, heartfelt letters, and surprise visits. Their love was the steady constant, anchoring them amidst life's tumultuous waves.

One evening, after a particularly draining day, Aarav sat in his sprawling office, looking out at the city lights. His phone buzzed with an incoming call – Elena.

"Hey," she began, her voice soft.

"Hey, love," Aarav responded, fatigue evident in his tone.

Elena sighed, "It's been tough for both of us, hasn't it?"

"It has," Aarav admitted. "But every time I think of you, every time I remember why I'm doing all this, it becomes worth it."

Elena smiled on the other end. "I've been thinking, Aarav. About us, our future. Where do we go from here?"

Aarav paused, contemplating. "We build, Elena. Together. I want you by my side, in every decision, every step of the way."

As the conversation deepened, the two began charting out plans for their combined future. It was clear that the journey ahead, while challenging, held the promise of shared dreams and boundless possibilities.

While Aarav and Elena dreamt of building a life together, unbeknownst to them, shadows from Elena's family history were creeping in, threatening to engulf their present in darkness.

Late one evening, while Aarav was working late in his office, a mysterious envelope arrived for him. There was no return address. Opening it, Aarav found a photograph. It was an old black and white picture, showing a younger version of Elena's Abuela, surrounded by a group of formidable-looking men, with stacks of money and firearms evident in the background. At the back of the photo, a note was scrawled: *"Every rose has its thorn. Know her past before planning a future."*

Chills ran down Aarav's spine. The message was clear. Someone wanted him to know about Elena's lineage. Aarav hides it in the drawer not paying attention to it right now.

It was evident that someone from the shadows of their families' intertwined histories was trying to drive a wedge between them. But who? And why now?

Stanford's hallowed halls witnessed an evolution. If the first year was about Aarav and Elena finding their rhythm as individuals, the subsequent years saw them seamlessly blending their worlds, intertwining their dreams.

Aarav managed a delicate balance between academia and his corporate responsibilities. His mornings were dedicated to video conferences, board meetings, and critical business decisions. Afternoons saw him at Stanford, engrossed in lectures, participating in debates, and working on research with Elena.

Despite the vast empire he now helmed, Aarav entrusted the daily operations of Mehta Enterprises to a handpicked team of experts, ensuring the company thrived in his semi-absence. This allowed him the luxury of time – time he wanted to spend learning, evolving, and being with Elena.

Elena, for her part, blossomed both in her academic pursuits and in her role as Aarav's pillar of strength. Her research papers began making waves in the world of international relations, and she took on the role of a guest lecturer for a few modules. The students adored her, not just for her brilliant insights, but also for her humility and approachability.

Their evenings were sacred, reserved exclusively for each other. Whether it was collaborating on their latest paper, enjoying a quiet dinner in town, or simply cuddling on the couch with a movie, the pair were inseparable.

One evening, after an intense study session, Aarav looked up from his notes, his gaze fixed on Elena. "You know," he began, "it's fascinating how our lives have merged. It's like we're two rivers that have met, becoming one powerful force."

Elena smiled, "And together, we're unstoppable."

He grinned, pulling her close. "Absolutely. With you by my side, I feel invincible."

"And I, with you, feel cherished," Elena whispered, resting her head on his chest.

Their shared life was a testament to the power of love, ambition, and partnership. Challenges, no matter how formidable, seemed surmountable. And as they charted their path forward, the future shimmered with promise and endless possibilities. Not all is bliss, The duo's fairytale existence took a dark turn one fateful evening. Elena past which was closely linked to abuela past was back, claiming everything they have built, together.

* * * * *

Part IV

UNRAVELING THREAD

The sun kissed the horizon as Stanford's iconic Hoover Tower gleamed under its golden hue. Aarav was seated in the library, engrossed in a business proposal, when his phone vibrated. Seeing Elena's name light up the screen, he immediately picked up.

"Aarav," her voice quivered, "I think... I think I've stumbled onto something."

He instantly snapped to alertness, "What is it?"

"My Abuela... there's more to her story than I knew. She was connected to the Cartel in Mexico." The weight of that revelation echoed in the silence that followed.

Aarav took a deep breath. "Okay, start from the beginning."

Elena explained her discovery, how a forgotten old photo of her Abuela with a man of significant power in the Cartel's hierarchy had set her on a research spree. The man, known as 'El Lobo', was now leading the Cartel, having recently usurped power.

"He's trying to legitimize his operations, Aarav. And from what I've gathered, he's interested in expanding his influence beyond Mexico. The connection to us... it's not just about my Abuela; it's about accessing your business empire."

The weight of this revelation was not lost on Aarav. The intertwining of their worlds, the academic and the business, had now taken a menacing turn. Aarav's thoughts raced. They needed a plan. He thought of the security measures he had already implemented and realized they needed more.

"We need to meet," he said, determination clear in his voice. "Stay in your dorm, lock everything up. I'm coming."

As Aarav raced through the campus, his mind raced faster. The Cartel was no small adversary. But he also knew that facing challenges was what they did best — together.

When he reached Elena's dorm, he found her surrounded by papers, trying to piece together more of her family's history. She looked up, her eyes filled with a mix of fear and determination.

"We're going to get through this," he whispered, pulling her into a comforting embrace. They stayed like that for a moment, drawing strength from one another.

Pulling back, Aarav looked deep into Elena's eyes. "We have resources, connections, and we have each other. We'll face this threat head-on, and we'll win."

The night was filled with strategic discussions, safety measures, and contingency plans. The Cartel had unwittingly awakened a formidable team in Aarav and Elena. Their love, combined with their unique skills, was a force to be reckoned with. The battle lines were drawn, and they were ready.

* * * * *

The morning sun found its way into the sprawling lecture hall of Stanford's international relations department. Prof. Mitchell, known for his expertise in North American geopolitics, took center stage. He began detailing the year's research topics, noting how they would shape the understanding of international relations in today's volatile environment.

As the list went on, Elena exchanged a glance with Aarav. They both knew what topic they had in mind. When the professor mentioned the influence of Mexican cartels on international relations, they exchanged a quick nod. Their personal dilemma had presented them with the perfect academic exploration.

After class, they approached Prof. Mitchell to discuss their project idea further. "We're particularly interested in the topic of Mexican cartels," Elena began. "We believe there are layers to this issue that haven't been fully dissected in the academic realm."

Aarav added, "Especially how these cartels use legitimate business fronts internationally to launder money, exert influence, and extend their power dynamics beyond borders."

Professor Mitchell looked intrigued. "It's a challenging topic, undoubtedly. But if approached methodically, you could shed light on a significant aspect of North American geopolitics. I approve."

As they left the hall, Aarav mused, "This research will not only benefit our academic pursuits, but it'll also provide us insights into our current situation. We'll be hitting two birds with one stone."

Elena looked worriedly at him, "I just hope we're not biting off more than we can chew. The deeper we dive into this, the more dangerous it might become."

Aarav gently squeezed her hand, "Together, we can handle anything. And we've got resources at our disposal, remember? Our research might just lead us to the information that could protect us and dismantle the cartel's operations."

As days turned into weeks, their dorm rooms were filled with a maze of papers, charts, and scribbles on whiteboards. They interviewed experts, combed through classified documents, and made connections. With every piece of information they gathered, they grew more knowledgeable about the Cartel's operations — and more resolute in their mission to stop its influence on Aarav's business empire and Elena's past.

But they also knew that with knowledge came risks. The deeper they ventured into the Cartel's world, the more eyes would be on them. And they had to be prepared for every eventuality.

When the clock strikes midnight Aarav heads out to get some McDonalds for them. Elena still engrossed in her research. As she glanced at her phone, a name flashed that she hadn't seen in years: "Mateo." Her heart raced as she hesitated for a moment before accepting the call.

"Mija," the voice dripped with a deadly sweetness that sent shivers down Elena's spine. "It's been so long, hasn't it? I hear you're doing well at Stanford."

Elena swallowed hard. "Mateo, what do you want?"

He chuckled, a sound devoid of any warmth. "Always straight to the point. I want to meet you. There are... matters we need to discuss."

"Why should I even consider it?" she challenged, trying to mask the fear in her voice.

"Because," Mateo replied slowly, "if you don't, things might not end well for your precious Aarav."

Elena's heart plummeted. "How do you even know about him?"

"I've always kept tabs on you, mija," he whispered menacingly. "It's what I do. So, tomorrow evening, the old café by the coast. You remember? Come alone. And remember, if I even get a hint of Aarav, it'll be his last day."

He ended the call, leaving Elena panicked and terrified. Every logical part of her told her to inform Aarav, but the very real threat against his life held her back. She was trapped in a dangerous web, a pawn in a game much bigger than she had ever imagined.

That evening, as the sun cast a fiery orange hue over Stanford, Aarav found Elena sitting alone on the grass, lost in thought. He sat down next to her, sensing something was off. "Hey," he said softly, "What's going on?"

She looked into his eyes, debating whether to share or keep her fears bottled up. The weight of the secret was too much, and tears welled up in her eyes. "Aarav, I'm so scared."

He held her close, promising to protect her. But even as they sat there, he could sense that Elena was battling demons from her past that were suddenly, and dangerously, becoming a very real threat in their present.

* * * * *

LOVE'S HIGH STAKES

The next day dawned with a feeling of unease for Elena. Her mind raced with the thought of meeting Mateo. She had known him in a different lifetime, one where she was naive and unaware of the depths of darkness that existed in the world. But now, she was changed, stronger and more resilient, yet still fearful of the memories that clung to her.

She had spent the better part of the night formulating a plan. It was risky, but she felt she had no choice. She would never forgive herself if anything happened to Aarav because of her past.

They met for lunch in Aarav's dorm as usual. Elena had managed to get some sleeping pills from a friend. She crushed them finely and, with trembling hands, mixed them into Aarav's drink. The guilt weighed heavily on her heart, but the thought of him getting hurt because of her was unbearable.

As they chatted about their morning, she watched him intently, waiting for the tell-tale signs of drowsiness. Aarav, oblivious to her internal turmoil, spoke about their research and the direction he wanted to take it. He noticed she was quieter than usual but attributed it to the stress of their project.

Halfway through the meal, Aarav's eyes began to droop. He shook his head, trying to fight off the sudden fatigue. "I don't know why I'm feeling so tired," he mumbled, his words slurring slightly.

Elena's heart clenched with guilt. "Maybe you should rest for a bit," she suggested softly.

He nodded, letting out a yawn. "Just a quick nap," he murmured, leaning back on his bed.

As he drifted off, Elena gently brushed the hair off his forehead and planted a soft kiss. "I love you," she whispered, the words spilling out for the first time. Tears pricked her eyes as she looked at him, hoping with all her heart that she was making the right decision.

Taking a deep breath, she grabbed her bag and left the dorm, making her way to the old café by the coast to confront her past and protect her future.

The seaside café seemed to have crystallized in time. With walls worn down by the relentless salty winds, it sat at the edge of the coast, cradling memories of yesteryears within its rustic embrace. Faint murmurs from bygone eras seemed to emanate from its corners, carrying stories of lovers, dreamers, and wanderers who had once sought solace under its roof.

As Elena pushed open the weather-beaten door, the café enveloped her in a dim, amber glow, reminiscent of old photographs that hold onto colors of memories long past. The quiet hum of an old radio added to the sepia-toned atmosphere, its melancholic tune speaking of longing and times gone by. With each step, the creaking wooden floor seemed to groan, echoing the weight of her apprehensions and the magnitude of the history she shared with the man waiting for her.

In the shadowed corner, away from the few rays of sunlight that managed to pierce the room, sat Mateo. His buzz-cut hair, the fierce intensity of his gaze, and the intricate tattoos etched onto his skin, each narrating tales of his allegiance to the cartel, marked him out. Time may have moved on, adding lines to his face and perhaps steeling his heart further, but his presence still commanded attention, pulling Elena into the vortex of their shared past.

He looked up as she approached, his lips curling into a sly smirk. "Mi dulce Elena," his voice was velvety yet hinted at the danger lurking beneath, and his smile, though seemingly warm, lacked sincerity. It was a smile that knew too many secrets.

Summoning strength she wasn't sure she possessed, Elena responded with a simple nod. "Mateo."

The atmosphere in the café thickened as Mateo's eyes drilled into her, his scrutiny feeling almost palpable. The juxtaposition of the tranquil seaside and the looming threat before her made the setting even more surreal.

A sardonic smile traced his lips. "Look at you," he mused, letting his eyes wander over her in an unsettling manner. "All grown up and polished. The naive girl I knew has been replaced with this... refined woman."

Swallowing hard, she steadied her voice. "Cut to the chase. What do you want?"

Mateo leaned in, the playfulness in his eyes replaced with a dangerous gleam. "Simple. Complete access to Aarav's empire. I want it all — data, contacts, pathways. In exchange, your loved ones remain untouched. And that pretty boy of yours," he sneered the last words, "stays breathing."

"Why drag Aarav into our past?" she challenged, though her voice trembled slightly.

His grin turned icy, revealing the depth of his resentment. "His wealth presents opportunities. But you? Your closeness with him? That's personal. You might have forgotten, but I remember every moment. Every betrayal."

Elena's memories flashed back to a time of chaos and danger, of passionate arguments and Mateo's obsessive love. "You still harbor resentment for a past choice?"

His answer came not in words, but in action. On the table, he played a live feed showing her family members — their everyday activities, their homes, their vulnerabilities laid bare. The message was clear: he had eyes everywhere. Especially on the little cousin she so dearly loved.

"You've got thirty days, mi dulce," he whispered, his voice both a threat and a caress. "And remember, involve the authorities or breathe a word of this to Aarav, and there will be consequences."

The walls of the old café seemed to close in on her, trapping her between a perilous history and an uncertain future, where every step she took could alter the course of her life with Aarav. The die was cast, and there was no turning back.

Elena's steps echoed on the pavement as she made her way back to Aarav's dorm, the weight of the evening bearing down on her. The orange-tinted streetlights cast an eerie glow, making her surroundings appear otherworldly. Every shadow seemed to move and whisper the name she had tried so hard to forget: Mateo.

Their history wasn't one for the fairy tales. The two of them grew up together in the same small neighborhood in Mexico, their homes separated only by a winding alleyway. As children, they shared stolen candy, secret hideouts, and a myriad of dreams. Elena would often dance under the moonlit sky, with Mateo playing a rustic guitar, the two dreaming of a world beyond their humble surroundings.

But as they grew older, their paths diverged. Elena pursued education, fueled by her abuela's aspirations for her. Mateo, on the other hand, was lured by the allure of power and quick money. He became involved with the local cartel, initially running errands but soon climbing the ranks.

Their adolescent love was tested when Elena discovered bags of cocaine hidden in Mateo's guitar case. The same guitar he played for her under the moonlit nights. The confrontation that followed was explosive and marked the end of their innocent love story.

She had hoped that was the end of their shared journey, especially after he was arrested for drug trafficking. The news of his arrest was both a relief and a heartbreak. Elena had hoped he'd find his way out of the darkness and back to the dreams they once shared.

But tonight, the ghosts of their past had resurfaced, reminding her that escaping one's history was never straightforward. As she reached Aarav's dorm, she felt torn between the world she left behind and the one she so dearly wished to build. Would she be able to protect her future with Aarav from the demons of her past? Only time would tell.

Elena knocked lightly on Aarav's door. Before she could turn the knob, it swung open, revealing a heated Aarav, his phone pressed tightly against his ear. His expressions were a mix of frustration and concern.

"No, you listen to me! That deal was solidified last week. It should've been finalized and executed by now! You had one job," he snapped, his voice laced with an authority that made it clear he was in charge.

Elena took a deep breath, reminding herself that this was a side of Aarav she needed to understand, especially given his new responsibilities as CEO. Approaching him, she placed her hands gently on his tense shoulders, massaging them in an attempt to alleviate some of the evident stress.

Aarav briefly glanced back, offering her a weak smile. The momentary break gave him enough calmness to finish his call, "Sort it out and get back to me with an update. And it better be good news."

He hung up, running his fingers through his hair in exasperation. Elena continued her ministrations, gently squeezing his shoulders and planting a soft kiss on his cheek. "Tough day?" she murmured.

"You can say that," he sighed. "This is the downside of running a business empire. One mistake, and the dominoes can start to fall."

She leaned against him, wrapping her arms around his waist from behind. "Whatever it is, I'm sure you'll handle it. You always do."

He turned around to face her, gently cupping her face in his hands. "Thanks, Elena. That means a lot. It's just... there's so much at stake now."

Elena gave a small smile, "Hey, together, remember?"

Aarav nodded, his forehead resting against hers. "Always." The silent comfort of the moment enveloped them, with the worries of their individual worlds temporarily kept at bay.

Little did he know about the storm that Elena was hiding from him. The secrets of her past with Mateo and the cartel's demands weighed heavily on her heart. But for now, she chose to keep them locked away, fearing how Aarav would react and the dangers it might put him in.

* * * * *

MUMBAI MIRAGE

The days flew by in a flurry of academic demands and hours spent in the library. As their research on the international implications of drug cartels deepened, Elena couldn't help but be reminded of the looming shadow Mateo cast over her life. Each fact they unearthed, every source they consulted, seemed to echo with the weight of her own personal history, blending with her desperation to save her family and keep Aarav safe.

One evening, while the two were pouring over some data at Aarav's dorm, Elena hesitated for a moment before offering, "You know, Aarav, maybe we could take our research to the next level. Why don't we travel to Mumbai? I've read that there's some strong data available on international drug cartels there. Plus, it might be good for you to see your father now that he's getting acquitted for Raghav's case. It might offer some closure."

Aarav looked up, surprise evident in his eyes. "That's... unexpected. But you're right. Seeing my father might bring some closure. And if it can aid our research, why not? Though, it's a bit out of the way. Are you sure?"

Elena nodded, her face impassive, hiding the turmoil inside. "Yes. Real-life experiences sometimes offer more insights than just textual data. Plus, it would be good to understand the Indian perspective on our topic."

Aarav looked thoughtful for a moment. "Alright. I'll arrange for our tickets and accommodation. We'll make it a short trip, focused on our research."

Unbeknownst to Aarav, the wheels in Elena's mind were turning rapidly. Going to Mumbai presented an excellent opportunity for her to discreetly access the information Mateo demanded. But it also meant deceiving Aarav, the one person who had shown her nothing but love and trust. It was a dangerous game, and Elena was caught in the middle.

* * * * *

Fast forward, Elena and aarav reach Mumbai. Mumbai's bustling energy greeted them the moment they stepped off the plane. The sounds of car horns blaring, the sight of brightly colored billboards, and the myriad of scents ranging from delicious street foods to the intense humidity was a sensory overload.

Upon their arrival at the opulent Mehta bungalow, they were greeted by household staff, moving efficiently, their demeanors respectful and welcoming. Aarav's mother, Mrs. Meena Mehta, a graceful woman in her fifties, welcomed them with open arms. Her saree, a magnificent piece of art with intricate embroidery, complemented her regal aura.

"Elena, dear," Meena said warmly, taking Elena's hands into her own. "It's wonderful to see you again."

Elena smiled, "Thank you, Mrs. Mehta. It's a pleasure to be here."

After some chit-chat and refreshments, Meena leaned in, "Elena, tomorrow we have a grand party to celebrate my husband's acquittal and to formally introduce Aarav as the new CEO. Everyone who's anyone in Mumbai will be there. I was thinking, perhaps you'd like to shop for some traditional Indian wear? The boutiques here have some exquisite pieces."

Elena's eyes sparkled with excitement, "That sounds wonderful, Mrs. Mehta. I'd love to."

The following day, Elena and Meena embarked on a shopping expedition. Mumbai's luxury boutiques were a world apart from anything Elena had experienced. She was draped in sarees of various hues, their fabrics soft as whispers against her skin. Meena, with her impeccable taste, helped Elena choose a beautiful emerald green saree, adorned with gold embroidery, saying it would complement her complexion perfectly.

As the evening approached, the Mehta mansion transformed into a scene of opulence. Crystal chandeliers cast their glow on the elite of Mumbai society. The air was thick with the scent of expensive perfumes, and the soft melodies of a live band played in the background.

Elena, in her saree, looked radiant. Aarav couldn't help but gaze at her with pride and adoration. The night was young, filled with laughter, music, and celebration.

But in the shadows, Elena's heart raced. With each passing hour, she was one step closer to executing her plan, to betraying Aarav for her family's safety. The weight of her secret threatened to suffocate her, even amidst the glittering grandeur of the party.

* * * * *

In the dimly lit study, Aarav and his father, Mr. Rajan Mehta, sat across from each other. The room was filled with the fragrant aroma of Rajan's favorite imported cigars, and the expensive mahogany desk bore witness to countless decisions that had shaped the Mehta empire.

"Aarav," Rajan began, taking a drag from his cigar, "we've been getting anonymous tips. The cartel isn't just focusing on their usual activities. They've got their eyes on our empire."

Aarav leaned forward, "How do we know this?"

Rajan took a moment, then replied, "A trusted contact in the police informed me that the cartel's been hunting for an insider. Someone who can give them an edge over us, help them infiltrate our systems, perhaps even our financials."

Aarav felt a pang of dread. "But we've always been careful. Our security, both digital and physical, is top-notch."

Rajan sighed, "No fortress is impenetrable, son. Especially when there's a possible traitor within. We need to be vigilant."

The weight of the situation pressed down on Aarav. "Who could want to betray us? After everything we've been through, especially with Raghav..."

Rajan interrupted him, "That's the problem with power, Aarav. It doesn't just attract allies. It attracts enemies. Many who wear masks of friendship."

Later that night, Aarav found himself at Raghav's grave. The tombstone, ornate and glistening under the moonlight, was a stark reminder of the fragility of life and relationships.

"Raghav," Aarav whispered, his voice filled with emotion, "why did it come to this? We could've been unbeatable together. Brothers side by side. Now, I'm left to protect our legacy alone."

The wind rustled the trees, a mournful lullaby for the past. Little did Aarav know that the threads of betrayal were weaving a new story, a story where Elena, the love of his life, found herself ensnared in the web of danger and deceit.

* * * * *

LUMINOUS DAWN

The Mehta residence was ablaze with lights. Ornate chandeliers adorned the grand ballroom, reflecting off the polished marble floors. Golden drapes framed vast windows, through which one could see the glittering Mumbai skyline.

Elena stepped out of her room, dressed in a stunning emerald-green saree. The delicate golden embroidery shimmered with every step she took. Her hair, braided with tiny golden beads, cascaded down her back. The makeup was subtle yet highlighted her striking features. A touch of kohl accentuated her deep brown eyes, making them even more captivating.

Aarav, wearing a royal blue sherwani with intricate golden patterns, couldn't help but stare. His heart swelled with pride and love. "You look breathtaking," he whispered, offering his arm.

She smiled, taking it. "Thank you. You clean up pretty well yourself," she teased.

As they descended the grand staircase, the guests turned their attention to the couple. Murmurs of appreciation spread through the crowd. It was evident; they were the center of attraction.

Aarav introduced Elena to a series of acquaintances, friends, and business associates. Among them were his childhood friends, Nikhil and Sana, who had stories about young Aarav that made Elena laugh.

An elegant woman, dripping in diamonds, approached them. "Aarav, my dear! It's been ages," she cooed.

"Mrs. Kapoor," Aarav greeted with a nod. "Allow me to introduce Elena."

Mrs. Kapoor examined Elena from head to toe, a hint of a smirk on her lips. "Quite a catch, Aarav. Well done," she commented, before sauntering away, leaving Elena slightly uncomfortable.

Throughout the evening, Aarav and Elena danced, laughed, and enjoyed the lavish party. But amidst the gaiety, Elena's mind kept drifting back to the dangerous deal with Mateo. The weight of her secret hung over her like a dark cloud, even in this world of glitz and glamour.

The announcement of Aarav's father's acquittal and Aarav's formal introduction as the new CEO was the highlight of the evening. There was thunderous applause, countless handshakes, and pats on the back. It was clear that the Mehta dynasty was a force to be reckoned with, and Aarav, at its helm, was poised for great things.

Amidst the cacophony of congratulations, Elena watched Aarav. She noticed the subtle strain in his eyes, the tightness in his smile. It was a huge responsibility, and while she knew Aarav was more than capable, she also understood the immense pressure he was under.

As the crowd dispersed, Elena made her way to Aarav. "Hey," she whispered, taking his hand. "How are you feeling?"

Aarav glanced down, the weight of the moment evident. "Overwhelmed," he admitted. "But it's a good kind of overwhelmed. Thank you for being here."

Elena squeezed his hand. "Where else would I be?"

It was then that Aarav's father approached them, his face glowing with pride. "Son, you were fantastic," he said, placing a hand on Aarav's shoulder.

"Thanks, Dad," Aarav replied, his voice choked with emotion.

Turning to Elena, Mr. Mehta added, "And Elena, it's wonderful to have you here. Aarav speaks so highly of you."

Elena smiled. "Thank you, sir. It's an honor."

After some more mingling and final words of congratulations, Aarav whispered to Elena, "Want to get out of here?"

She nodded. "More than anything."

The duo discreetly exited the grand ballroom, leaving behind the world of business deals and corporate politics. They stepped into the cool Mumbai night, the city lights sparkling like a million stars. The night was still young, and the city's magic awaited them.

The streets of Mumbai were alive even at this late hour. The city, which seemed to never sleep, was aglow with lights, sounds, and a distinctive energy. Aarav navigated through the streets with the ease of someone who had grown up amidst the city's chaos, leading Elena to a quaint ice cream parlor.

"Rustom's!" Elena read the name aloud, the retro sign glowing warmly.

Aarav grinned. "Best ice cream in town. An old Parsi joint. You'll love it."

They walked in, and the aroma of freshly baked waffle cones wafted through the air. The menu was vast, with flavors ranging from traditional to eccentric. Elena chose a scoop of roasted almond, while Aarav went for his childhood favorite, Sitaphal (custard apple).

With their ice creams in hand, they made their way to Marine Drive. The iconic boulevard stretched endlessly, the Arabian Sea on one side and the glittering city skyline on the other. They found a quiet spot and sat down, the gentle sea breeze cooling their faces.

Elena took a bite of her ice cream and let out a sigh of contentment. "This is divine."

Aarav chuckled. "Told you."

They sat in silence for a while, enjoying their ice creams and the hypnotic rhythm of the waves crashing against the rocks. Every now and then, a car would zoom past, leaving a trail of light in its wake.

"I used to come here a lot," Aarav began, breaking the silence. "Whenever things got too much at home or school, I'd find solace here. It has a calming effect, don't you think?"

Elena nodded, leaning into him. "It's beautiful. I can see why it's your favorite spot."

They spoke about their dreams, their fears, and their hopes for the future. The conversation flowed seamlessly, as if they had known each other for a lifetime. The city's noises faded into the background, and all that remained was the two of them and the vast expanse of the sea.

As dawn approached, Elena rested her head on Aarav's shoulder. "Thank you for bringing me here, Aarav. Tonight was magical."

Aarav wrapped an arm around her. "Anytime, Elena. With you, every moment is magical."

The streets were nearly empty as they drove back to Mehta's bungalow. The anticipation between them was palpable, a current of electricity in the air. Pulling up to the grand entrance, they climbed out of the car. The bungalow was shrouded in a soft glow from the exterior lights, casting gentle shadows across the elaborate gardens.

Once inside, Aarav locked the door behind them, the audible click a harbinger of what awaited. Elena could feel her heart racing, each beat echoing in her ears. Their eyes locked, a mix of passion and vulnerability present in both their gazes. Wordlessly, Aarav led her to his room, the weight of their shared experiences and the present moment pressing on them.

In the dim light of the room, their hands met. Fingers intertwined, they stood inches apart, breathing in the scent of each other. Elena's fingers traced a path up Aarav's arm, over his shoulder, and finally came to rest on his face. The intimacy of the moment was electrifying.

Gently, Aarav leaned in, capturing Elena's lips with his. Their kiss was slow, deep, full of raw emotion. They explored each other, each touch a revelation, a statement of love. Their clothes became barriers to the closeness they sought, and soon layers were shed, revealing two souls in their most vulnerable state.

Aarav whispered against her ear, his voice husky with emotion, "I love you, Elena."

She responded, her voice filled with equal passion, "I love you too, Aarav."

They moved together, each motion an echo of their emotions. There was no rush, no urgency, just two souls connecting on a profound level. The world outside ceased to exist. There was only them, their love, and the room that held their secrets.

Hours seemed like moments, and as the night turned to dawn, they lay wrapped in each other's embrace, the events of the night a testament to the depth of their love.

The morning sun's rays crept into the room, painting them in a soft golden hue. In that serene moment, all worries and fears were forgotten, replaced by the comforting warmth of being loved and being in love.

* * * * *

The Shattered Mirror

The morning sun filtered through the intricate curtains of the study, casting a soft glow on the polished mahogany desk. The room was still, with only the faint hum of the computer breaking the silence. Elena stood in front of the large wooden door, taking a moment to gather herself before entering. She knew the risks of what she was about to do, but the threats Mateo had made were real and imminent.

She remembered the code Aarav had used the day before and quietly entered it. The door clicked open, and she quickly slipped inside, shutting it behind her. The study was filled with shelves of books, trophies, and artifacts from around the world, but her focus was on the state-of-the-art computer sitting on the desk.

She booted it up and quickly accessed the company's mainframe. Her fingers danced across the keyboard, searching for the files Mateo had demanded. Her heart raced as she inserted her pendrive and began transferring the critical data.

Outside, the house was beginning to wake up, with faint sounds of movement and distant murmurs carrying through the corridors. Elena's pulse quickened, knowing she was running out of time.

Just as the last file was about to finish transferring, she heard footsteps approaching. Panic surged through her, and she quickly ejected the pendrive, shutting down the computer. She was about to slip out the same way she came in when the door opened. It was one of Aarav's servants, looking puzzled to see her there.

"I thought I heard a noise," he said, surveying the room. "Is everything alright, ma'am?"

Elena, her heart pounding, managed to conjure up a calm facade. "Oh, yes. I was just looking for a book Aarav mentioned. Sorry if I disturbed anything."

He nodded, still looking a bit suspicious but saying nothing more. Elena, clutching the pendrive tightly in her hand, made a swift exit and headed back to the room.

Back in the sanctuary of their shared space, she quickly hid the pendrive and took a few moments to steady herself. The weight of her actions pressed heavily on her conscience, but the safety of her family and the love she felt for Aarav were driving forces that couldn't be ignored.

All she could hope for was that the consequences of her betrayal wouldn't shatter the world they had built together.

* * * * *

The airport was buzzing with activity as Elena hurriedly navigated through the crowds. The weight of the pendrive in her pocket felt like a ton, and her heart ached with every step she took away from Aarav and the life they had built together. She booked a last-minute flight to Mexico City and found herself waiting at the gate, her mind racing with the gravity of her decisions.

She kept replaying their last night at Marine Drive, the raw emotion, the depth of their connection. How could she betray someone she had grown to love so deeply?

She had left a hastily penned letter for Aarav:

Dear Aarav,

I wish there were words to explain the turmoil within me right now. But no matter how much I try, words fail to convey the depth of my sorrow and regret. I never meant for any of this to happen.

Mateo, my past, came back haunting me, threatening our future. He has leverage over my family, over people I love dearly. The choices I made were driven by fear and desperation. I had to protect them, even if it meant betraying you.

I've taken the data he demanded. It was the only way to ensure their safety. I wish I could have explained everything to you face-to-face, but I feared for your life, for our love, for everything we have.

I'm flying to Mexico, hoping to put an end to this nightmare. I want you to know that everything I did, I did out of love – for my family and for you.

Always and forever,

Elena.

As the flight took off, Elena leaned back, tears streaming down her face. She was caught in a storm of emotions, a whirlwind of love and betrayal. She clutched the letter close, praying that Aarav would understand and that they would find their way back to each other.

In Mumbai, Aarav woke up to an empty bed. The lingering warmth where Elena had slept was the only reminder of their night together. He found her letter on the dresser and, as he read through her words, a tidal wave of emotions crashed over him. He felt anger, confusion, pain, and beneath it all, an undying love for Elena without wasting a second he changed and left for the airport

The Mumbai airport had never felt more intimidating to Aarav. With every step he took towards the private jet awaiting him, his resolve grew stronger. He was about to step into a world of danger and uncertainty, all for the love of Elena. The weight of the loaded gun against his back was both a reassurance and a constant reminder of the risks involved.

His tech team, a highly skilled group of individuals he trusted implicitly, had provided him with the exact coordinates of Maeto's location in Mexico City, along with real-time tracking of Elena's flight.

As his jet sped through the sky, Aarav used the time to strategize. He reviewed all the information he had on Maeto, his operations, and the locations he frequented. The objective was clear: get to Elena before she handed over the data and found herself in deeper trouble.

Upon landing in Mexico City, Aarav wasted no time. The bustling streets, full of life and vibrant colors, were a stark contrast to his grim mood. He drove through the city, tracing Elena's steps, until he reached a heavily guarded mansion in the outskirts.

Elena, in the meanwhile, had just arrived at Maeto's hideout. The weight of what she was about to do bore down on her, making her feel both nauseous and light-headed.

"Mi pequeña rosa," Maeto's voice was a low drawl, a chilling reminder of a past she wished to forget. With shaking hands, Elena handed over the pendrive, praying that the shadows of her past would finally release her family.

Maeto's fingers brushed hers, deliberately lingering, sending a shiver of revulsion through Elena. "Did you think this would be enough, querida? A mere trade?" His eyes, dark and calculating, darted to the pendrive.

Just as he was about to plug it in, the sounds of a distant explosion made them both jump. Gunfire erupted outside, shouts and screams piercing the thick walls of the hideout. Maeto's guards ran amok, trying to contain the sudden attack.

Elena's heart raced. This was her chance. She lunged at Maeto, both of them wrestling for control over the pendrive. But for all her determination, Maeto's physical strength was hard to combat. His fingers closed around her wrist, squeezing tight, his other hand readying to strike her.

Suddenly, a gunshot silenced the room, and Maeto's grip went limp. Elena, panting and shaken, pushed him off to see him crumple lifelessly to the floor.

Standing at the doorway, gun still smoking, was Aarav. His hair was disheveled, sweat and dust smeared across his face, but his eyes—those intense eyes—were fixed on Elena. His gaze was a blend of fury, concern, and a fierce protectiveness she had never seen before.

In two strides, he was by her side, his arms encircling her protectively, shielding her from the chaos outside. The intensity of the moment was palpable. The dangerous dance of love, betrayal, and redemption had bound them even tighter. Their future was uncertain, but for now, they were together, amidst the ruins of the past.

With Maeto's lifeless body sprawled on the floor, the gunshots and commotion outside began to die down. The cartel members, realizing their leader's demise, streamed into the room, weapons lowered, and a sense of uncertainty in the air.

Aarav, keeping Elena behind him protectively, stepped forward, his face illuminated by the dim lights. The heavy silence was a testament to the sheer dominance he exuded. The cartel members exchanged nervous glances, the power dynamics shifted entirely within a matter of minutes.

Suddenly, one of the senior members, a tall, burly man with a prominent scar across his cheek, dropped to one knee. "Señor Mehta," he began, his voice carrying a grudging respect. One by one, the rest followed suit, bowing their heads in submission.

Aarav raised his hand, signaling for silence. "The past is the past," he began, his voice firm yet measured. "I want no war, no bloodshed. But understand this, I will do whatever it takes to protect what's mine. Respect this new boundary, and we can coexist."

Elena watched, awestruck, as Aarav showcased a leadership style that was both assertive and diplomatic. This wasn't the same young man from Stanford; this was a leader, a protector, a king amongst men.

With a nod, the senior member responded, "You have our allegiance, Señor Mehta." There was a unanimous murmur of agreement from the others.

Aarav turned to leave, pulling Elena close to him. As they made their way out, he whispered, "It's over, Elena. We're safe now."

Back at the Mehta mansion, Aarav recounted the harrowing events to his family. As he spoke, the room was thick with tension. Every word he uttered was weighed down by the weight of the truth, the realization of the dangers they had faced, and the web of deceit Elena had been caught in.

His amma, always the pillar of strength and discipline, let her emotions show. Her eyes flashed with worry and anger as she reprimanded Aarav. "How could you be so reckless? Taking on the cartel? What if something had happened to you?"

Aarav lowered his head, regret and exhaustion evident on his face. "I had to, amma. I couldn't let Elena face this alone. Despite everything, I still care about her."

His father chimed in, "You've always had a strong sense of responsibility, Aarav. But sometimes, you need to think about the repercussions. The cartel isn't something to be taken lightly."

Aarav's gaze hardened. "They kneeled to me. The Mehta name now commands their respect. I've secured our position, and they won't dare cross us."

The revelation was met with stunned silence. The enormity of what Aarav had accomplished, combined with the risks he had taken, left the family grappling with a mix of pride and fear.

Amidst the family turmoil, Aarav's academic life didn't stand still. He and Elena, even in their strained relationship, worked diligently on their thesis. Their topic, once just an academic pursuit, had now become their lived reality. Their combined experiences lent a unique perspective to their research, making their submission one of the most talked-about papers at Stanford.

However, the events in Mexico had cast a long shadow over Aarav and Elena's relationship. While he respected her commitment to her family, Aarav couldn't shake off the sense of betrayal he felt. He needed time, time to heal, and time to reevaluate the depth of their bond.

Elena, on her part, felt the growing distance between them. While she had acted out of desperation to save her family, she realized that some wounds took longer to heal. She missed the closeness they once shared but respected Aarav's need for space.

The end of the academic year approached, and with it came a period of introspection and decisions for the future. Would Aarav and Elena find their way back to each other? Only time would tell.

* * * * *

THE CRUCIBLE OF CHOICES

The summer sun of Stanford streamed through the windows, illuminating Elena's room in a warm glow. She sat there, staring at the tiny plastic stick in her hand. Two distinct lines stared back at her. There was no denying it. She was pregnant.

A whirlwind of emotions engulfed her - happiness, anxiety, fear, and hope. This was a life-altering moment, and she was experiencing it alone, without Aarav by her side. Deep down, Elena had hoped that this shared responsibility might be the catalyst to bridge the growing chasm between them, but she was unsure if it was the right time to break the news.

She remembered their moments together, their dreams, and their plans. The times they talked about a future, children, and a life filled with love. But, at this moment, all of that seemed like a distant memory. The present was complicated.

Elena tried approaching Aarav multiple times over the next few weeks. She'd wait for him after classes, trying to catch a moment to talk, but he'd always be surrounded by friends or rushed off to some meeting. Every time she got close, something held her back from revealing the truth. The fear of his reaction, of rejection, of not being supportive plagued her mind.

Meanwhile, Aarav, despite his firm resolve, found himself constantly thinking about Elena. Late at night, he'd find himself scrolling through their old pictures, remembering their happy times. However, the hurt and betrayal always crept back in, pushing him further into his shell.

One evening, as Aarav was heading out of a lecture hall, he noticed Elena sitting alone on a bench, her face buried in her hands. His first instinct was to walk away, but something held him back. He approached her cautiously.

"Elena?" he called out softly.

She looked up, her eyes red and puffy from crying. The sight of her in such a state tugged at his heartstrings.

"What's wrong?" he asked, genuine concern evident in his voice.

Elena took a deep breath, mustering the courage to speak. "Aarav, we need to talk."

Elena looked deep into Aarav's eyes, searching for a sign of the man she had fallen in love with. "Aarav," she began hesitantly, "there's something you need to know."

Aarav's expression remained guarded, but something in his gaze softened. As Elena took a deep breath and whispered, "I'm pregnant," Aarav's walls slowly started to crumble. The weight of her words, so unexpected and monumental, bore into him. For a long moment, there was silence, the air thick with tension and a multitude of unspoken emotions.

Then, in a gesture that surprised them both, Aarav gently reached out, cradling Elena's face in his hands, and pressed a tender kiss to her forehead. It was a kiss filled with a whirlwind of emotions: surprise, confusion, tenderness, and a hint of the deep love that still lingered between them.

Drawing back, he met her gaze, his eyes shimmering with unshed tears. "We'll figure this out," he whispered, echoing her sentiments. "Together."

As days turned into weeks, the weight of their situation pressed down on them. The responsibilities that came with Aarav's empire, both legitimate and not-so-legitimate, seemed even more significant with the knowledge of the life growing inside Elena.

Yet, amidst this chaos, the allure of the world's largest senior MUN presented an opportunity for both Aarav and Elena to make a difference on a global scale. A chance to work with the UN was a dream they had both shared, and now it held even more significance.

Their relationship, once a beacon of passion and understanding, had been strained to its limits. But with the revelation of their impending parenthood, they faced an even more complex tapestry of emotions. They had challenges ahead, but there was a glimmer of hope that love, understanding, and time could mend their bond.

Can Aarav balance the immense pressures of his dual roles? Will Elena and Aarav be able to traverse the complexities of their relationship to shine at the MUN? What does the future hold for their child? With time marching forward, the answers to these questions remained shrouded in the mysteries of the future.

* * * * *

www.ingramcontent.com/pod-product-compliance
Lightning Source LLC
LaVergne TN
LVHW041158150826
845673LV00001B/201